FACE TO FACE WITH PERIL...

Slocum ignored Barrett, hoping he would go away, but the deputy had his claws dug in, and he wasn't going to leave until he ripped a little flesh.

"You know, Slocum, I've seen dozens of hardcases like you. And not one of them wasn't sorry he was such a bigmouth by the time he left here. I got a feeling you ain't gonna be no different."

Slocum clenched his fists involuntarily, and Barrett laughed.

"Go ahead, you sonofabitch, hit me. It'll be the last thing you ever do." Barrett jabbed the muzzle of his shotgun into Slocum's belly. "You ever seen a man been gut-shot, Slocum? It ain't a pretty sight. And he's a long time dyin'. So go ahead, just give me an excuse..."

OTHER BOOKS BY JAKE LOGAN

JAKE LOGAN

SLOCUM AND THE CROOKED JUDGE

B

BERKLEY BOOKS, NEW YORK

SLOCUM AND THE CROOKED JUDGE

A Berkley Book/published by arrangement with
the author

PRINTING HISTORY
Berkley edition/April 1989

ISBN: 0-425-11460-0

A BERKLEY BOOK ® TM 757,375
Berkley Books are published by The Berkley Publishing Group,
200 Madison Avenue, New York, N.Y. 10016.
The name "BERKLEY" and the "B" logo
are trademarks belonging to Berkley Publishing Corporation.

PRINTED IN THE UNITED STATES OF AMERICA

10 9 8 7 6 5 4 3 2 1

1

John Slocum reined in, his horse fighting to keep from slipping on the rocky scree under its hooves. From the top of the rise, he could just make out the ramshackle skyline of a small town. The buildings were mostly shadow, just visible against the gray filling the valley below. Turning in the saddle, Slocum looked back over his shoulder at another valley. Like this one ahead of him, it was dry, its edges lined with shattered rock, its broad bottom full of sand and fifty kinds of cactus, three or four of which he knew by name. Beyond the town, whatever the hell it was, he knew there was another valley just like it. And beyond that lay another, then another.

The town would have to do until civilization stumbled through the high desert. At least he could find a saloon. With any luck, there might even be a hotel, someplace to sit down in hot water, let his aching back rest against the smooth copper tub. And if he really got lucky—he was tempted to say, if there was a God in heaven—he might even find somebody soft, somebody willing to rub his shoulders and lie down with him for as long as it took to get back the feel of a woman's flesh under him. As unlikely as that prospect seemed, he could still hope.

Slocum yanked his canteen free and unscrewed the cap. The lid grated with a sandy scratch, a sound as dry as the terrain. The horse snorted, smelling the little water left in the canteen, then skittered sidewise. Slocum patted the big roan before wiping the grit from the mouth of the canteen. He tipped his hat back, then tilted the canteen. His knuckles went white, as if he were trying to squeeze a little more water out of the battered tin. A small trickle, coppery in the fading light, dribbled out, and he shook the canteen once before accepting its emptiness.

He patted the horse again while slip-knotting the canteen back over the saddle horn. Kicking gently, he nudged the roan up over the crest of the ridge and into the loose soil on the down slope. A faint trail, the same one he'd been following for three days, slashed across the face of the slope in a series of switchbacks. The big stallion, almost dainty in its careful gait, navigated the trail cautiously, now and then dislodging a small rock or two. Every little stone seemed to gather a few more as it rolled and then slid over the sandy face of the ridge, a hiss of sand trailing along behind.

The trail gradually flattened out, and Slocum kicked the roan into a fast trot. Man and horse were both bone tired. The sun began to sink behind the town, smearing the hills with orange light. In the distance a purple smear on the horizon, the San Francisco Mountains, caught fire for a few moments before the sun slipped down behind it. The town twinkled, half its buildings showing light in a window. The trail grew rutted, the twin gullies worn by countless wagon wheels warning Slocum to keep a sharp eye peeled.

The buildings themselves were little more than blocky shadows now against the deepening purple of the mountains and fire-edged indigo clouds. On the right, a splintered sign, nailed to a fence rail sunk in the ground, told him he was approaching Flat Creek. The town's name had been painted in a wavy hand, small trickles of black paint making the letters look foreign. The population, if the sign were to be believed, was a modest two hundred and seven. Slocum wondered what could have kept that many people in so godforsaken a place.

On the edge of town he found a livery stable. Its faded red paint was peeling away to reveal the dead gray of old timber underneath. Slocum dismounted in front of the high double doors. Inside, he could see a mound of hay and a few still-unbroken bales. The soft glow of a kerosene lantern threw a wavering shadow across the hay, and Slocum called hello as he tugged his roan toward the stable. His spurs jingling, he hollered again, this time louder, and poked his head through the open door. The sickly sweet smell of damp hay and horse manure filled his nostrils.

As he entered, he saw a tall, thin man in a checkered shirt, the owner of the shadow, stab an old pitchfork, its handle worn smooth as bone, into one of the hay bales. While the fork still quivered in the bale, the man tugged a pair of dirty leather gloves free and tossed them onto the hay next to it.

"You open?" Slocum asked.

The man turned suddenly. Catching sight of Slocum, he reached for the lantern and lengthened the wick before answering, "Wouldn't be here if I wasn't. What can I do for you? Rent or stable?"

"Stable," Slocum said. "How much?"

"How long?"

"I'm not sure."

"Then I'm not either." It could have been a smart answer, but the man smiled too easily. He jerked his thumb toward a battered sign on the inside of the closed door. "By the week's cheaper. Three dollars. The day rate's okay too —six bits—but you stay four days, you might as well pay the week." He laughed, then said, "It's up to you, young fellow."

Slocum looked more closely, then realized the man must be older than he appeared. The smooth, leathery skin of the man's face, half hidden under a whitish stubble of beard, had the look of an old saddle.

"Two days'll be fine," Slocum said, digging in his pocket for the money.

"Suit yourself." The old man stuck the coins in his own pocket. "You want a receipt?"

"Do I need one?"

"Nope."

"There a hotel in town?"

The old man crooked his thumb toward the door. "Flat Creek Hotel, up the street, over the saloon of the same name."

"Thanks," Slocum said, then led the roan all the way into the stable. He uncinched the saddle and draped it on an empty stall, then tugged the blanket free, shook it out, folded it, and tucked it under the saddle. He left the reins on for the old man. "See you in a couple of days."

The old man nodded. "I'll be here."

Slocum stepped out into the street, his legs a bit wobbly under him. Three days in the saddle had left him a little shaky. Two buildings down, a boardwalk started, and he nearly tripped as he climbed the single step. A rickety ramada, held up by splintered poles, ran the length of the boardwalk. The hard wood under his heels echoed in the deserted street. A few doors ahead, a bright yellow rectangle spilled out onto the sandy street, where the doors of the Flat Creek Saloon hung open.

Slowly regaining his stride, Slocum paused at the open door for a moment, sizing up the clientele before stepping on through. At the bar, he ordered a whiskey, insisting on the genuine article, and dropped a dollar on the bar. The bartender slapped a thick empty glass on the polished wood, tilted a labelless bottle into the glass, then walked away. Not friendly, but not unfriendly—he was just going about his business. Slocum tossed the shot down, caught the bartender's eye, then turned to watch the room.

A poker game attracted his attention, and he watched a big red-haired man, his faded blue denim shirt rolled nearly to his shoulders, riffle the cards. The dealer was rawboned, his skin a dark copper. The shirt wrinkled under a pair of broad suspenders but was taut across the biceps. The guy was big, but he wasn't fat. From the look of him, Slocum guessed him to be a farmer.

The others were workingmen as well. Two cowboys, still wearing their chaps, sweat-stained Stetsons tilted back on their heads, sat opposite one another at the big round table. The fourth man was dressed like a farmer, but he didn't look the part. His back was to Slocum, but the skin of his neck was too pale to be that of a man who made his living out under the sun. The game was small stakes, stacks of small coins balanced precariously in front of each man.

When the dealer had finished shuffling, he pushed his chair back and stood up. Slocum put his height at a shade over six feet. Ambling toward the bar, he flashed a friendly grin Slocum's way. He nodded, then bellied up to the bar and called the barkeep.

"Hank, gimme a round, will ya?"

"Same all around?"

"Why change now?"

Hank laughed and drew four beers, swept the foaming heads with a thick wooden stick, then clustered the mugs in a semicircle, handles toward the farmer. "Here you go, Randy. On the tab?"

Randy nodded. He started back toward the poker table, then paused to look over his shoulder at Slocum. "Care to try your hand? We could use some new blood. Things are pretty dull."

"Thanks. Don't mind if I do."

Randy grinned, shifted the mugs to indicate he wanted to shake hands, and hollered past Slocum to the bartender. "One more on the tab. Okay, Hank?"

Drawing a fifth beer, Hank quickly beheaded it and slid the mug toward the front lip of the bar. Slocum caught it by the handle and nodded his thanks. He followed Randy to the table and waited for the introductions before pulling up a chair. The two cowboys were cousins, Travis and Dan Calder. Slocum introduced himself, and the cowboys nodded.

The fourth man just stared with a flat, expressionless face. His close-set, slightly crossed eyes looked as if they resented the bridge of a narrow nose, the only thing keeping them apart. His name was Clay Barrett. Hairy, thick-knuckled hands skittered nervously on the tabletop in front of him. Even when Randy, whose last name was Carter, began to deal, the restless hands strayed back to the small stacks of coins after picking up each card. They reminded Slocum of wolf spiders, the way they pounced on each card then dashed back to the coins.

There was something unsettling about Barrett. He was even bigger than Randy Carter. That he was a local deputy was anything but reassuring.

"Where you from, Slocum?" Travis Calder asked.

"Georgia, originally. Anywhere but, lately."

"Johnny Reb, huh?" Carter asked, his voice on the edge of laughing. Ignoring Slocum's silence, he continued, "I was on the other side, myself. Hundred and Third Pennsylvania. Never got to Georgia, though. I hear it's pretty."

"Used to be," Slocum said. "But I don't like to talk about it."

Fine by me," Carter said. "It's best forgotten, anyhow." He glanced at Slocum, and realized there wasn't a chance in hell of that ever happening.

"Why don't you just tend to your cards, Carter?" Barrett barked. "You been gabbing all night."

"Just making friendly conversation, Clay." Carter sounded hurt more than intimidated.

"Well, don't." Barrett jerked two cards from his hand, folded the remaining three in one hairy fist, and discarded. "Gimme a pair."

They played in near silence for a half hour, the deal passing from Carter to Travis Calder and then to Barrett. Slocum could feel the big man's eyes on him from time to time, but each time he looked Barrett's way, he ducked his head into his cards. Slowly but surely the distribution of the coin stacks began to shift. Barrett was winning small amounts, but winning steadily.

Slocum began to pay closer attention. A friendly game had become something altogether different. Cheating didn't make any sense, not in a game where the stakes were the very definition of penny-ante, but Slocum was convinced that Barrett was somehow cheating. He glanced at the other players, to see whether they seemed to notice anything, but if they had, they weren't bothered by it.

Slocum stood up slowly, raking the balance of his stake toward the edge of the table. "I think I better tend to getting myself a room."

"Quitting already?" Carter asked.

"Luck seems in short supply tonight," Slocum answered.

"You ain't the only one can say that," Travis volunteered.

"I ain't doing too bad," Barrett said. His voice was as neutral as his expression.

"I can see that," Slocum answered.

"Stranger in town, seems like he ought to stay in a friendly game," Barrett continued. "You never know, you might need some help before you leave."

"I generally look after myself pretty well," Slocum said.

The faintest suggestion of a smile tugged at the corners of his mouth.

"Course, some people, they don't give a damn about manners. Hospitality, that sort of thing."

"You been hospitable, all right," Slocum said. "But there are some times when it don't pay to be a guest."

"What are you saying?" Barrett demanded.

"Take it easy, Clay," Travis said. "Slocum don't mean nothing. He dropped a little coin. Maybe he ain't used to it. Maybe he ain't got too much to lose." He reached out and patted Barrett on the arm.

Barrett shook him off. "A man can't afford to lose, he shouldn't be playing cards. Not with me, anyhow."

"You can say that again," Slocum said.

"Now hold on. You say I'm cheating, Slocum?"

"He ain't saying nothing like that, Clay," Carter said.

Barrett pushed back his chair and got to his feet. "You think I'm cheating, don't you, Slocum?" He balled his fists and leaned across the table.

"I'll tell you exactly what I think," Slocum said. "I think I'm going to get myself a room upstairs. I'm tired and I need a bath. That's what I think."

"You need more'n that. That's what *I* think." Barrett lunged across the table, reaching for the front of Slocum's shirt. The thick fingers slid down the front of the shirt, popping a button. Barrett, his weight too far forward, lay sprawled across the table.

In the sudden silence, the button, still spinning on edge on the floor, sounded like approaching thunder. Barrett slid off the table. As he tried to regain his balance, he was distracted for a split second, and Slocum took full advantage. He stepped in and drilled the bigger man with a quick combination, slamming a hard left into Barrett's midsection and a quick right cross to the side of the jaw. Slocum pulled the second punch, hitting Barrett just hard enough to send him tumbling backward. Before he could rise, he was grabbed by the Calder cousins. He struggled in their grasp, but they each grabbed a handful of shirt and hung on.

"That didn't have to happen, Barrett," Slocum said.

"But it did happen, you bastard, and it ain't finished." From the seat of his pants, he continued to snarl up at Slocum, who turned his back and walked toward the hotel desk. "You ain't seen the last of me. Bank on it."

Slocum ignored him, and signed the register.

2

Handing the clerk two days' rent for the room, Slocum waited for the key. "And I'll want a bath, too," he said, as the clerk pushed the heavy iron key across the desk blotter.

"You mean you're dirty, too?"

Slocum turned slowly. When he saw her, he was glad he did. A stunning redhead, her figure just short of exploding through the fancy gown, its lace shoulder straps at half mast, grinned at him.

Slocum grinned back. "I can be," he said.

"I'll bet. I'm Karen Alston. I didn't catch your name." Her voice was husky, with just a hint of calculation in the breathy contralto.

Two months of riding fence in West Texas is like two years anyplace but hell. Slocum hadn't seen a woman in nine weeks. He wasn't sure he'd ever seen one like Karen Alston. He studied her a long moment before answering. In the back of his mind, a little voice kept telling him to be careful not to say the wrong thing. This one was too good to let get away.

Broadening her grin just a bit, she adjusted the rose in her décolletage. As a gesture designed to call attention to her full breasts, it was completely unnecessary.

Slocum smiled. "Thornless, I hope."

"Me or the rose?"

"Do you have to ask?"

"A girl likes to know what a man's thinking."

"Miss Alston, I'm barely thinking at all."

She took a step, then leaned forward to snatch the key dangling impotently from his fist. "I'll show you to your room, Mr. . . . ?"

"Slocum. John Slocum."

". . . Mr. Slocum. Follow me."

She turned and started up the stairs. Mesmerized by the sway of her hips, Slocum followed. "You work here?" he asked.

On the second-floor landing she turned and smiled. "In a way," she said. "In a way."

The thick carpet on the hall floor muffled their steps. Karen led the way with an easy confidence. At the door to number five, she turned and offered him the key. "You can open it yourself."

Fumbling with the key, Slocum watched her with one eye, as if fearful she would vanish the moment he stopped looking at her. He finally found the keyhole and pushed the door open. It banged into the wall with a dull thud. Karen Alston brushed past him, closer than necessary. She paused long enough for him to be aware of the pressure of her breasts on his arm, waited an extra beat, then vanished into the dark interior of the room.

Slocum followed her in, closing the door behind him. He heard the clink of glass on glass as a match rasped on a striker, sparking once then dying. The sharp sting of phosphorus filled the room. The match scraped again, this time flaring into life. In its glow, he could see Karen Alston bent over a kerosene lamp, her bare shoulders washed a pale orange by the flickering flame. The glass clanked again as Karen replaced the chimney. The orange glow gradually turned pale yellow. She adjusted the wick, and the lamp smoked momentarily. When she had it to her satisfaction, she turned to Slocum, still just inside the closed door. She half leaned and half sat on the heavy walnut table, her gown ballooning out around her.

"That should be bright enough." She smiled. Then, with an exaggerated pout, she continued, "Unless you want to read."

"Not unless I have to."

With an easy grace, she regained her feet, then walked toward Slocum, changing course at the last minute to step around him.

"You're not leaving, are you?" he asked.

Without looking at him, she said, "Not unless I have to."

"You don't."

"Then I won't." The statement was punctuated by the grating of the lock as it snapped shut. Reaching up slowly, she grasped his hat by the brim and pulled it off. Then she tossed it into a far corner of the room. Then, walking around behind him, she encircled his waist and fumbled with the heavy buckle of his gunbelt. "You won't need this for a while," she whispered.

When the belt was free, she walked to the table and, coiling the belt around the holster, placed it gently, almost reverently next to the lamp. Her fingers hesitated, then, as if unaware she was being watched, she caressed the butt of the Colt Navy. "Are you good with this?"

"Good enough."

She seemed not to have heard him. She turned to face Slocum, her face expectant.

He didn't disappoint her. Stepping in close, he bent and kissed her upturned mouth. Her sweetly scented breath hissed through slightly parted lips, then turned to a sigh as she opened her mouth still further. His hands slid across the bare shoulders, then snaked under the tight cloth just beneath her shoulder blades. Her broad back was solid, the flesh tight and well muscled. The skin was so smooth, he wasn't sure it was she or the satin dress beneath his fingers. She pressed into him, sliding her own hands down to his hips and pulling him toward her.

"You do need a bath," she whispered.

He was about to respond when a sudden knock echoed through the room.

"Damn," Slocum hissed. Then, louder, he hollered, "Who is it?"

"It's me sir, Virgil. Your bath is ready."

Slocum reluctantly disengaged himself. "Just a minute," he called. Releasing the lock, he opened the door with an impatient jerk.

Virgil, a steaming pail in each hand, stood in the hall. He smiled at Slocum, then turned sideways to duck-walk through the doorway. The water sloshed noisily in the pails, some splashing over the lips of the pails and darkening the carpet. Virgil set the pails on the floor and hurried back into the hall.

A moment later, the blunt end of a tub appeared in the doorway, followed by a grunting Virgil. The unwieldy copper monstrosity rolled and skidded intermittently. When the tub was in the center of the room, he stepped on the brake lever. "Just to make sure she don't roll on you, Mr. Slocum."

Then, one after the other, he emptied the two heavy pails of water into the tub with a thin metallic thunder. Grabbing the empty pails, he rushed out, calling over his shoulder, "I'll be back in a minute."

Slocum looked at Karen and shrugged. She laughed. "It couldn't hurt. You *do* have a certain fragrance about you."

"His timing could be better."

Before she could answer, Virgil was back, this time with two pails of unheated water. He set them down beside the tub. "I'll let you decide on the temperature."

"Much obliged, Virgil." Slocum reached into his pocket

and pulled out a dime. Virgil accepted it with a bow and a hurried thank you, backing through the door and closing it again.

Slocum followed him, locked it, then turned back to Karen. "Now, where were we?"

Instead of answering, she reached behind her back and, with a rustle, unhooked the gown, letting it fall to the floor. She grinned. "We were about to take a bath, weren't we?"

"I thought women wore all kinds of things under a dress like that," Slocum said.

"Live and learn, cowboy."

Karen eased toward him, her breasts thrust forward, jiggling with each step. Slocum started on his shirt, stripped it off, and tossed it to one side. He unbuttoned his pants and stepped out of them. Stiff with trail dirt, they stood nearly knee high. Karen daintily kicked them to one side, and Slocum couldn't take his eyes off the curve of her instep. Until she raked one red nail down the center of his chest, stopping just below the belt.

She tested the water. With one hand, she lifted one of the buckets of water, poured half of it into the tub, then replaced the pail on the floor. The gesture was so smooth and easily done, Slocum found himself wondering how a woman could look so soft and be so strong.

"Get in, Mr. Slocum," she said.

Somehow, he had the sense he shouldn't refuse, even if he wanted to. Stepping into the high-backed copper tub, he felt the hot water to his knees, then slowly lowered himself, letting the warmth slowly climb his legs and lower torso. An indented soap dish sported a new bar of unscented soap, and he reached for it, closing his fingers over the bar just as Karen's hand got there.

"I'll take that," she whispered.

Slocum acquiesced. Karen knelt by the side of the tub, her breasts supported by the cold metal rim. She reached down into the water to wet the soap, then slowly lathered him, starting at the bottom and working up. Her fingers were strong, kneading his tired muscles as she worked. He wondered how she had come by the skill, or whether it was a natural gift. He felt the trail ache soaking out of his tired body. Carefully, almost prissily, she ignored his genitals, moving swiftly from waist to shoulders.

She seemed almost detached, absorbed in her work. She bit her lower lip as she concentrated, almost as if she were unaware of his presence. He watched her face, the passivity of her expression, until she scooped water from the bath and doused his hair. Closing his eyes, he felt her fingers work through his tangled hair, rubbing the soap deeply into hair and scalp alike. Then suddenly, she was gone. He was about to call out when a torrent of cool water cascaded over his head and shoulders. He shook his head, spluttering as the water ran into his mouth.

Then, before he could shake free of the water, he felt her hand on his cock. Expertly, she lathered, bringing him to parade dress in short order. Long after he was soaped clean, she stroked, her grip alternately tight and lax, as if she could sense when he was too close to ejaculation.

He opened his eyes, but she stopped just long enough to press the lids closed. "Never mind, just feel. You don't have to look." Afraid she might stop, he did as he was told.

He felt her change position, then, with a sudden shock, felt a different kind of warmth envelop his rigid penis. The slickness, the scalding heat, told him, but he opened his eyes anyway. The grin on her face was brighter than the lamp behind her. Her knees were up near his shoulders, pinning him to the high back of the tub. Suddenly still, she squeezed him. Then, ever so slowly, she started to rock, taking him still deeper inside herself, rising until he thought she would expel him altogether then rapidly plunging back down. As with her hand, she seemed sensitive to his state, slowing her rhythm from time to time, to prolong the coupling.

The smile, frozen on her face, was as stiff as he was. It was devoid of passion, as if she knew what he was feeling but felt nothing herself. It was close to contempt. Struggling against her weight, Slocum started to move his hips, accelerating the pace. Like wax too near a flame, her wintry smile began to melt, and soon she relaxed, letting him call the tune, like a gifted dancer suddenly confident in her new partner.

Faster and faster Slocum moved. Broader and broader her smile became. He stared at her, losing himself in the deep green eyes. She licked her lips, then clamped down on her tongue, its pink tip just visible between clenched lips. He slid soapy hands to her hips, controlling her motion completely now, lifting her then sliding her back down. Each time she rose, he backed away, each time he pulled her close, he arched his own hips. She started to pant, then her mouth opened slowly and she moaned.

He was in command now, and she followed his lead, like a newly broken mare under an experienced rider. Letting his hands slide higher, he cupped her breasts and felt the rigid nipples under his thumbs. He slowed his pace, and she took the hint. He massaged her breasts, then leaned forward to take one pink nipple in his mouth. He sucked harder, ignoring the bitter soap, letting his teeth nibble at the erect nipple.

She moaned louder, then bucked furiously, trying to goad him into a rapid rhythm. Her urgency made her impatient. He let the nipple slip from his mouth and pulled her head down. He looked at her for a long moment, then kissed her. Her tongue flamed into his mouth, and he responded with an acceleration of his hips. Each time he drove into her depths, he held her for a moment, straining to go still deeper. She cried out, then collapsed. Her head lay on his shoulder, and he could feel her teeth nibbling at his ear. Her breathing was rapid and shallow.

When she spoke, her voice was hoarse. "Ever had a ride like that, cowboy?"

Slocum said nothing. Exhausted, he fell back, letting his breath come in long, rasping pants. She used her muscles to keep him hard, undulating slowly but careful not to let him slip free. With a long, tantalizing movement of her hips, she backed away. Slowly, he felt himself begin to wilt. When he slid out of her, the hot water of the bath felt cool on his skin. She climbed out of the tub, sloshing water onto the carpet, then backed away, toward the bed. She reached behind with her left hand, found the thick towel, and rubbed herself with languorous strokes.

Satisfied, she lay back on the bed, one long leg bent at the knee. She spread her legs and slipped one hand between them. "Let's try again."

Slocum stood up in the bath, and she tossed him the towel. Stepping onto the carpet, he bent to dry himself, when he heard the lock snap open. He turned as the door burst inward.

"What the hell . . . ?"

Clay Barrett stood in the door, a Peacemaker in one clenched fist. He stepped into the room, kicking the door closed behind him. Keeping the gun leveled on Slocum, he crossed the carpet in three quick strides. Karen started to reach for a folded blanket, but Barrett caught her wrist with his free hand. Yanking her to her feet, he smacked her sharply across the face. She fell backward, but he caught her and hit her again, this time with clenched fist.

Slocum dove at the big deputy, but Barrett was too quick for him, slashing the Colt in a vicious arc. The gun struck him on the temple and Slocum fell to the floor, groggy. Barrett brought back his foot and kicked Slocum in the face as he struggled to rise.

Slocum lay on the floor, staring at the elaborately tooled leather of Barrett's boot. Then everything went black. He heard Karen cry out again, then lost consciousness altogether.

3

Slocum woke up with a monster headache. He tried to open his eyes, but the light was too painful. He closed them again, and tried to acclimate himself by feel alone. The hard stone underneath him was a far cry from the carpet he remembered. Feeling the side of his head, he winced when his fingers touched his temple. A lump the size of a small egg still oozed watery blood.

He tried to get to his knees, but his head throbbed with the effort, and he lay back down. Shaking his head slowly, he groaned. Opening his eyes to slits, he turned in the direction of the light. Through the narrowest of slits, he could see a brilliant oblong some distance overhead. Opening his eyes a little more, he realized the dark vertical bands through the oblong were bars. The rest, he could imagine.

Getting to his knees, biting his lower lip against the pain, he slowly straightened. Opening his eyes wide, he blinked away a haze, and the room began to spin. Propping himself up with stiff arms, he stared around the cell. He wasn't alone. Three men huddled in one corner, whispering to themselves and staring at him. He shook his head again and tried to stand.

"I wouldn't try that just yet." The voice was behind him, but he was sure he'd heard it before. He wanted to turn, but it hurt too much. A strong hand grabbed him under one arm and steadied him as he tried again. On his feet, still shaky, he realized the room was starting to spin, and he shut his eyes again to ward off the vertigo.

Slocum didn't like feeling this vulnerable. He forced himself to move, turning slowly. He felt the hand, still gripping his upper arm, tense for a second, then, as he negotiated the turn, relax and finally let go.

Randolph Carter stood there, a quizzical half smile curling the corners of his mouth. "You feeling a little better?" he asked.

"I've felt worse, but not recently." Slocum wobbled a bit, and Carter reached out to steady him, this time content simply to brace the unsteady Slocum. "Am I where I think I am?" Slocum asked.

"Yup."

Slocum nodded, then slowly surveyed the cell. It was typical in almost every respect. Thick steel bars, rooted in mortar at top and bottom, enclosed the space along one wall. The remaining three walls were of mortared rock. Without examination, Slocum knew they were thick. Whoever had built it had known what he was doing, and what the room was intended for.

The single window, high on the outside wall, sported several bars of the same thickness. They were closely spaced. Even a child would have had trouble slipping between them. But the cell was not intended for children. Of that, there was no question.

A second cell, smaller but no less secure, stood next to Slocum's. Both featured a row of bunks with thin straw pallets instead of mattresses. The bunks were empty, and

Randy steered the still groggy Slocum toward a lower bunk in the corner against the wall.

"How did I get here?" Slocum asked.

"Don't you remember?"

"All I remember is getting slugged with a pistol. And kicked in the head."

"Clay Barrett said you attacked a woman, one of the hookers at the hotel."

"Bullshit! We were... well, you know what we were doing. And Barrett kicked the door in with his gun drawn. He slapped the woman, Karen, a couple of times, and when I tried to stop him, he cracked me across the head."

"That's not what Barrett says. And, for your information, that's not what Karen Alston says either."

"What?"

"She says you attacked her, and that Barrett stopped you."

"That's crazy! Why would she lie?"

"I can guess."

"I got the feeling there's something here I ought to know."

"You can say that again, Slocum."

"And what the hell are *you* doing in here?"

Carter looked embarrassed. He looked at the floor for a long minute, shuffled his boots on the hard stone, then turned to look out the window. "It doesn't make any difference, does it? I mean, I'm here, and there's nothing I can do about that."

Slocum grabbed Carter by the arm. "I want to know. Then we'll decide what we can do about it."

Carter snatched his arm away. There was surprising strength in the young man. Slocum inhaled deeply, held it for a long second, then let his breath out with a hiss of exasperation. "All right, if you don't want to tell me, I guess I can't make you."

Carter was about to reply when a clang interrupted them. Slocum looked toward a heavy steel door that separated the cellblock from the rest of the building. The door swung back and slammed into the wall behind it. Two cowboys were shoved roughly through the open door. Clay Barrett stood behind them cursing.

Barrett stepped through the doorway and shuffled lazily toward the cell. Another deputy, a shotgun cradled in one crooked elbow, stood in the doorway behind him. Barrett held a large steel key ring. The keys jangled as he walked, and he tapped them idly with an outstretched finger. Sitting on the bunk in the corner, Slocum watched the big deputy through hooded eyes. Barrett glanced at him once, but said nothing.

Opening the cell door, Barrett stepped back, tugged at the heavy door, and let its momentum carry it open. The only sound in the cellblock was the squeak of the heavy door on its thick hinges. Barrett backed away from the open cell door and tilted his head. "Get on inside, and make it quick." One of the two cowboys mumbled something, but Slocum couldn't hear what was said. If Barrett heard, he gave no sign.

When the two newcomers had entered the cell, Barrett slammed the door shut. The heavy metal tolled like a bell, its echo lingering long after the initial impact, the way the sound of a tuning fork slowly fades away. Deliberately, with obvious relish, Barrett inserted the key and relocked the cell door. He started to leave, then, as if on an afterthought, turned back and stepped close to the bars.

He looked directly at Slocum for the first time. "You comfortable, cowboy?"

Slocum ignored him.

"I hope you ain't *too* comfortable, 'cause you ain't going to be here too long. You hear me?" Barrett rapped the heavy ring of keys on one of the bars. "Slocum, you hear me?"

Slocum again said nothing.

"Why don't you leave him alone, Barrett?" Carter stepped close to the bars. Slocum stood up as Carter

grasped the bars on either side of Barrett. The deputy
sneered. "You never learn, do you, farm boy? If you could
mind your own business, you wouldn't even be in there.
But I guess some people have to learn things the hard
way."

He rapped Carter's knuckles sharply with the heavy
ring, and Carter yelped in pain. He let go of the bars and
cursed the deputy, who just laughed.

"You be good, now, boys, and I'll see you tomorrow.
All right?" Then Barrett turned and left. The thick metal
door resealed the cellblock. Slocum stepped to the bars and
stared after the deputy. Barrett, his face split in a broad
grin, watched him a few seconds through a small barred
window in the door. Then, with a casual wave, he was
gone.

Carter, sucking on his bruised knuckles, stepped back
and sat down on one of the bunks.

"What was that all about?" Slocum asked.

"Nothing. Just Barrett's style, I guess."

"Don't hand me that. What did he mean about you not
minding your own business?"

Carter ignored the question. Slocum sat down beside
him on the bunk, but Carter turned away.

"What's this," one of the newcomers asked, "a lovers'
quarrel?"

Slocum glared at him. "Shut your mouth."

"I thought farmers liked sheep, didn't you, Walt? But
maybe not. Maybe they like cowboys. Maybe this one
does, anyhow."

"I told you to shut up," Slocum snapped.

"I ain't talking to you, I'm talkin' to the sodbuster."

Carter stood up and stepped toward the cowboy. His
fists were clenched, and Slocum stood up to grab him. For
some reason the cowboys were baiting Carter. That meant
they were ready for a fight, even trying to provoke one.
Slocum was not one to meddle in someone's business, but

Carter had been friendly, and friends were in too short supply to stand by when one got in trouble.

"Farm boy thinks he's tough, Walt. Don't he?"

"Maybe he just likes you, Darrell." Walt was sliding casually to the left, while Darrell drifted slightly to the right. Carter was too angry to see the trap they were setting for him. If he went after Darrell, Walt would be able to step in from behind.

Slocum glanced at the three men in the corner, who had stopped whispering when Barrett came into the block. They were watching Carter intently. Walt, in a move so slight Slocum wondered whether he might have imagined it, nodded to the three, then took another step to the side.

"That right, farm boy?" Darrell laughed. "You like me better than your buddy? You want to kiss me or something?"

That was the last straw for Carter. He lunged toward Darrell, just slipping away from Slocum's outstretched fingers. Carter swung from the heels, too angry to do anything else. Darrell slipped the punch and landed a sharp right to Carter's ribs. Walt stepped in from behind and locked a thick arm around Carter's throat. Slocum grabbed Walt and tried to drag him away, but the man was wiry, and his grip around Carter's neck was too secure.

Slocum, still weak from his pistol whipping, threw a quick combination—a left, a right, and another left—landing three sharp blows just over Walt's kidneys. Walt let go of Carter and turned to see who had attacked him. Slocum stepped forward, but somebody grabbed his legs from behind and he fell heavily, landing on his side and striking his head on the stone floor. He turned in time to intercept a well-aimed kick just before it struck his ribs. The three men from the corner had either been there by design or had decided to take sides.

Slocum grabbed the foot, jerked sideways, and the man tumbled over him. Ignoring his throbbing head, Slocum scrambled to his feet. He ducked a punch from one of the remaining two, slammed the guy's chin with a right cross, then jerked him by the shirtfront and shoved him backwards. Grabbing the man by his shoulders, he shook him, then slammed his head into the bars. The man groaned and slid to the floor.

The third man backed away, shaking his head as if to signify that he was no longer interested in joining the fray. Slocum turned back to Carter, who had Darrell backed into a corner. Walt was reaching into his shirt, and his hand came away with a short, wicked-looking knife.

Slocum called to Carter, who turned just as Walt leapt forward with his arm outstretched. The knife sliced through Carter's shirt, and a thin smear of blood rapidly stained the frayed edges of the cloth. Darrell, seeing an opening, grabbed Carter from behind. Walt regained his balance as Slocum charged across the cell. Shifting his grip on the knife handle, Walt stepped toward the wounded man, while Darrell tightened his hold around Carter's throat.

Slocum intercepted the knife hand just as it started forward. He gripped Walt's forearm, stopping the attack, then spun Walt around. He turned his back and used his weight to slam Walt into the bars. Taking the knife hand in both of his own, Slocum brought it up, ducked under, and spun rapidly around. Slamming Walt face-first into the bars, he jacked the arm higher and higher until he heard a sharp crack. Walt moaned, and Slocum slammed him into the bars again, then let go. From the corner of his eye he caught a glimpse of Barrett watching through the small window.

With Walt out of commission, Carter was able to concentrate on Darrell. His face was red from lack of air, but he summoned the strength to drive an elbow into Darrell's rib cage. The powerful thrust exploded the air from Darrell's lungs, and he lost his grip on Carter.

Turning to face his adversary, Carter grabbed him by the shoulders and lifted him by brute force off the floor. He shook the smaller man the way a terrier shakes a rat, then tossed him to the ground. Carter reached down, grabbed Darrell by the shirtfront, and hauled him to his feet. He was about to drive a huge fist into Darrell's face when the door to the cellblock swung open.

Barrett, a shotgun held in one hand, stepped into the cellblock, a second deputy just behind him, also armed with a shotgun. "That's enough," Barrett barked.

Panting, Carter dropped Darrell to the floor, making no attempt to cushion his fall. "It was enough ten minutes ago. Where the hell were you then?"

Barrett grinned before answering. "Why, hell, Carter, I was havin' myself some supper. Keeping law and order is gettin' to be a mighty demanding job. A fellow needs his nourishment and he wants to do it right. Don't you think?"

"I think you set this whole thing up, that's what I think," Slocum said.

"I wasn't asking you," Barrett snarled.

"No, you weren't. But I'm telling you anyway."

"You got a smart mouth. You're lucky you're in there, Slocum."

"One of us is," Slocum answered.

"You think I can't take you anytime I want to? We'll see about that."

"I don't imagine you could take anybody who wasn't half naked."

"Now, now." Barrett grinned. "A man who don't watch the company he keeps can't be too fussy about what happens to him. I expect you'll learn that lesson tomorrow. Then we'll see just how smart you are."

He turned to the second deputy. "Davey, you better get those fools outta there. Let Slocum and Carter have a cell to themselves. Judge Bradley'll take it from here."

4

Slocum watched as Walt and Darrell were taken to the front of the jail, then vanished around a corner into the outer office. The remaining three men were transferred to the second cell, leaving him and Carter alone in the larger of the two cells.

You didn't have to be a scholar to see that the best laid of plans had fallen apart. For whatever reason, Walt and Darrell had been put in the cell to work Carter over. About the other three, Slocum was less sure. They might have been bullies, looking for some fun, or they might have seen which way the wind was blowing and decided to score a few points for themselves.

Slocum stretched out on one of the bunks, while Carter sat on the floor, leaning against the wall. It was late afternoon, and the sun had been heating the jail all day. The temperature must have been near one hundred degrees, and the slight breeze that managed to slip through the small window gave little or no relief.

Off in the distance, Slocum heard thunder. It rumbled

intermittently for nearly a half hour. He watched Carter the whole time. Since questioning the young farmer had been useless, he decided to sit it out. If asking didn't cut it, maybe silence would. Carter seemed unaware of his presence, staring at the floor mostly, once in a while lifting his gaze to the window high above him on the wall.

Once or twice he cleared his throat and Slocum thought maybe the silent treatment was about to pay off, but nothing happened. Instead, Carter just turned his head and spat through the bars, then went back to his daydreaming.

Slocum's head still ached. The rest of his body was slowly recovering, but the lump on his temple was still there, and still tender to his touch. His neck and ribs were sore too, and he knew he had been kicked at least once the night before, but his bruises no longer insisted he notice them. He was aware of the pain only when he moved suddenly.

The cowboys in the other cell were quiet now, as if their interest in Carter and Slocum had been just a passing fancy; once it left them, all sound and motion seemed to have gone with it. A bright flash of lightning slashed across the sky, throwing a hard-edged block of banded light on the cell floor. A moment later a tremendous crash of thunder rattled the bars. The sudden hiss of a heavy downpour started, and the sky quickly darkened.

Carter stood up and walked to the window. He grasped a bar with each hand and hauled himself up to look through the unglassed opening. He nodded slightly then let himself back to the floor. Slocum waited expectantly, but Carter resumed his seat and his silence.

The rasp of a lock being turned echoed in the cell, and Slocum turned to watch the door. It opened slowly, and a bulky shadow that could only belong to Barrett stepped through, followed by a smaller figure.

"You got a visitor, farm boy," Barrett said.

The shorter figure stepped closer to the bars, and lightning flashed again, illuminating the gloomy cell for a moment. In the brief moment, Slocum realized the visitor was a woman. Perhaps she was Carter's wife.

Slocum hoped not. She was full-figured, and long dark hair, soaked by the rain, framed a face that left little to be desired except a closer look. The next blaze of lightning revealed still more. A faded blue work shirt, also soaking wet, clung to a pair of full breasts. Stimulated by the cold rain, their nipples were clearly outlined against the wear-softened cloth. If she was wearing anything under the shirt, it hid next to nothing.

"Randy, are you all right," she asked. Her voice was soft, almost a whisper, but there was no disguising the concern she felt.

"I'm okay, Sissy, but you shouldn't be here."

"I was worried. When you didn't come home last night, I tossed and turned. I didn't fall asleep until daybreak, or I would have been here sooner."

"You shouldn't have come."

"Of course I should have. How could I not?"

"You can't do anything."

"I can get you out. How much is the fine?"

"What fine?"

"Well, that must be why you're here. Drunk and disorderly, something like that."

Carter didn't say anything. Lightning flashed again, and Slocum watched her face change in that brief instant as it dawned on her that matters were far more complicated than she had imagined.

"Well, isn't it?" she demanded.

"No, it isn't."

"Then what's going on?" She stamped her foot, like a kid being teased by a favorite uncle. "Tell me! How can I get you out of here?"

"We'll have to wait until tomorrow. I won't know until then."

"Why not?"

"That's when the trial is."

"Trial? You can't be serious. What did you do?"

Carter bowed his head and said nothing.

Barrett, standing in the open doorway, chuckled. "There's ways of gettin' him out, Sissy."

"I know all about your ways, Clay Barrett, and if you say that again, so help me, I'll shoot you. Shoot you dead."

"Now Sissy, you can't go threatening a peace officer. I might have to lock you up. And I'm sure them boys in the next cell must be bored. You'd be just the thing to amuse them for a while."

"Barrett," Carter hissed, "I swear to God, you even think about it, and I'll cut your heart out."

"Shut up, Carter. You're already in shit up to your neck. Beggin' your pardon, Miss Sissy, but it's the truth." Barrett bowed in a parody of gentlemanly apology.

"What's he done? What's going to happen to him?"

"I reckon you'll have to wait till Judge Bradley has his say tomorrow."

"Where is he? I want to talk to him."

"He's out at the ranch right now, as a matter of fact." Barrett's smile, lit by sheet lightning, was a ghostly blue.

The young woman turned back to Randolph Carter. "Randy, I'll get you out of there, I promise." Then she was gone, brushing past Barrett in her angry haste.

"Night, boys," Barrett said, giving them an ironic salute.

Carter watched as the door closed, his fingers curled around the bars. For a long time he kept staring at the locked door. An occasional flash of lightning would splash through the small window and spill over him. Slocum watched silently as the statue that was Randy Carter stood motionless. But the image that Slocum saw in the darkness was that of the young woman. He wanted to know who she was but was reluctant to ask Carter. It seemed certain that he would see her again. Slocum knew he couldn't wait.

The hiss of rain slowly died away, but the clouds lingered, and twilight gradually turned to darkness. Finally, Carter let go of the bars and shuffled to the bunk next to Slocum's. Slocum heard the creak of springs and the rustle of dry straw as Carter arranged himself on the pallet.

For several minutes, Slocum stared into the darkness, trying to see Carter's face, but the lumpy shadows against the wall were well out of reach of the scant glow spilling through the window. Finally, Slocum said, "I think it's about time you told me what's going on here, Randy."

Carter didn't answer.

Slocum sat up on his own bunk. "Randy, you hear me?"

Carter grunted.

"I got the distinct feeling," Slocum continued, "that somehow you're in here because of me. That right?"

Carter said nothing.

"Because if it is, I think I ought to know about it."

Carter maintained his stony silence. Slocum waited, finally lying back down on the bunk and folding his arms behind his aching head. After a half hour, Slocum tried a new tack. "Your wife's got a lot of grit."

A long moment later, Carter said, "I'm not married."

Slocum nodded in the dark. "Good night," he said.

Carter didn't answer.

Slocum felt a hand on his shoulder and shot up on his bunk. A man he'd never seen before was leaning over him. A shiny new deputy sheriff's badge glittered on the pocket of his shirt. "Time to rise and shine. Judge Bradley likes to sit before it gets too hot."

Slocum groaned. His head felt better, but his joints were stiff. In case he'd forgotten, bumps and bruises on every part of his body reminded him of the last two days. Carter was already awake, sitting on his own bunk.

The deputy indicated a pail of water on the floor. "You can wash up some before we leave. We're fresh out of soap, though."

Slocum knelt on the floor. Cupping his hands, he rinsed

his face with the tepid water. He dampened his hair and combed it out with his fingers. His mouth tasted like the sole of an old boot, but there was nothing he could do about it. Getting to his feet, he looked at the deputy.

Stepping back to let Slocum move through the door, the deputy said, "If you fellers are ready, let's get a move on."

A second deputy stood in the outer doorway, a shotgun cradled in his arms. Slocum had never seen him before either. In the hall outside the cellblock, Slocum turned to wait for Randy Carter, who moved slowly, as if in a daze. The hallway led straight out to the street, which still showed traces of the previous night's thunderstorm. There were no puddles, but the earth was dark, and only straw danced in the light breeze.

Randy Carter joined him, and, on the deputy's order, the four men stepped out into the deserted street. The deputy led the way across the street and up onto a wooden walkway, then made a right. Slocum saw the neat white sign, lettered in black with the words "Municipal Court" in a neat hand. The deputy turned in through a doorway under the sign, and Slocum followed.

He found himself in a large room, a simple wooden table at one end. A chair, obviously for witnesses, sat to the right of the table, facing the front door. A few backless benches, in neat rows, completed the furnishing.

Behind the table, a tall man with severe sideburns and a walrus mustache, all white, shuffled papers on the table-top. He was framed in an open doorway directly behind him. He looked up as the men entered, and Slocum realized he must be looking at Bradley. The judge nodded slightly, his impassive face almost biblical in its craggy immobility.

The deputies led Slocum and Carter to the front bench, then sat on the bench immediately behind them. Slocum eyed the judge curiously. Carter looked at his lap, where his fingers twined and untwined nervously.

The judge studied them minutely, his mouth slightly

curled with distaste. The old man's face was a deep bronze color, and coal-black eyes, threatening to burst into flame, shifted from Slocum to Carter and back again.

The judge reached for a gavel and rapped a wooden block on the table. Over the hollow thump, he rumbled, "Let's get on with it. Time waits for no man. And neither do I. Clay?"

Barrett strolled through the doorway behind the judge with an insolent strut. "All set, Your Honor," he said.

"Sit down, Clay." Bradley shoved a thick Bible, in a well-worn leather binding, to the end of the table closest to the witness chair. "You can swear yourself in. You know how."

Barrett did as he was told, then plopped into the stiff-backed wooden chair. It creaked beneath his bulk, but Barrett seemed not to notice. Slocum wondered how often he'd been through the routine.

"All right, tell me what happened." Bradley folded his hands on the table in front of him and cocked an ear in Barrett's direction.

"Well, sir, it's pretty straightforward. Slocum there— you know Carter, and the other one's Slocum—beat up on a lady night before last, over to the hotel. I caught him in the act, and he resisted arrest."

Bradley looked at Slocum. "You have anything to say for yourself, Slocum?"

Slocum fidgeted, then said, "Yes, Your Honor, I do. Looks to me like it's my word against his. And that just isn't what happened."

"Then suppose you tell me what did happen."

"I was in my room at the hotel when Barrett here busted in, he had a key, I think, and he started hitting a young friend of mine."

"This young friend didn't happen to be a woman, by any chance, did it?"

Slocum hesitated.

"Well, did it?"

"Yes, sir. It did."

"And what was the young woman's name, Mr. Slocum?"

"Miss Karen Alston."

"How well do you know this young woman?"

"Not well, Your Honor."

"Except in the biblical sense," Barrett snickered. "He knows her that way, all right."

Bradley ignored the deputy. "In fact, you had just met her that night, hadn't you?"

"Yes, sir."

"And she's not a friend at all, is she, Mr. Slocum? She's actually a harlot, is she not?"

"I'm sorry, Your Honor, I don't know the term."

"A prostitute. Isn't that what she is, Mr. Slocum?"

"No, sir."

"I remind you that perjury is a crime, Mr. Slocum."

"I understand that, but I didn't pay her any money, so it's not prostitution. And I didn't beat her. Barrett did."

Bradley leaned toward Barrett and mumbled something. The deputy stood up and disappeared through the door behind the judge, reappearing a moment later. He stood behind Bradley and waited. A moment later, Karen Alston stepped through the door.

She sat in the witness chair and placed her hand on the Bible. Bradley addressed her sternly. "Do you solemnly swear to tell the whole truth, so help you God, Miss Alston?"

"I do."

"Please speak up. I can't hear you. I remind you that this is a court of law, and the fate of two men hinges on your testimony."

"I do." This time she spoke loud enough for all to hear. Slocum noticed the edge of bitterness in her voice. When she lifted her chin to stare at the judge, Slocum was stunned. One of her eyes had been blackened, and it was swollen nearly shut. Dark smudges which he knew to be bruises traced her chin on both sides of her face.

"Do you know a man named John Slocum?"

"Yes."

"Do you see him in this courtroom?"

"Yes," she whispered. Then, slowly raising a quivering hand, she pointed in Slocum's direction. "That's him, on the right."

"And how do you know him?"

"He. . . . I was at the hotel, and I met him. He told me, I mean he . . . he asked me to . . ." She started to sob.

"All right, Miss Alston. Perhaps I can help you. He offered you money, didn't he, in exchange for engaging in fornication with him."

Karen nodded slowly. "Yes."

"And you did fornicate with him, did you not?"

"Yes."

"And when you wanted to be paid, he beat you until Deputy Barrett intervened, did he not?"

This time Karen just nodded in the affirmative.

"And when Deputy Barrett tried to arrest Slocum, Randolph Carter attempted to prevent it, did he not?"

The nod was barely perceptible.

"All right, Miss Alston, you may be excused." Bradley watched her stand and walk back through the door. When she was gone, Bradley leaned back in his chair. He stared at Slocum for a long minute. "I don't think I have to hear any more."

"No, I didn't think you would," Slocum said.

5

"Ninety days."

Bradley slammed the gavel down on the block, then tossed it cavalierly to the table. Slocum stared in disbelief. It was bad enough that Karen Alston had lied, but ninety days was an unbelievable sentence. Now Randolph Carter received the very same sentence, and all because he had refused to stand by and do nothing when a man he barely knew was being railroaded.

Bradley watched as Clay Barrett locked shackles around Slocum's ankles, then snapped a second set on Randolph Carter. The second deputy stood by, the ever present shotgun at half-mast. Slocum's hands were cuffed behind his back, then Carter's.

"Let's go, boys," Barrett said. He was gloating, and made no attempt to disguise the satisfaction in his voice. He took the shotgun and prodded Slocum with the muzzle, rapping the base of his spine harder than necessary.

Slocum turned, but before he could say anything, Bradley, observing from his seat behind the table, barked, "I think, Mr. Slocum, you'll find, on reflection, that you are already in enough trouble. I am a hard man, but a fair man. I wouldn't recommend that you make your sentence any more difficult than it already is."

Slocum turned to face the judge. "You call this fair? One man convicted on perjured testimony. A second for trying to prevent a miscarriage of justice. If this is your idea of fair, I'd love to know what you consider injustice."

"You know, Mr. Slocum, your type never seems to understand that the law applies to them. You like to think you are above the law, that it was meant for others, but not for you. But, I assure you, if you persist in your obstinance, you will find that I am more than your equal in tenacity."

"You want to see tenacity, Judge, you be here when I get out. I'll really show you something."

Nothing burned Slocum more than thievery masquerading as the law. He had seen more than his share of chicanery. His family's land had been lost to a bunch of bastards about as interested in truth and justice as Clay Barrett was. He had returned home after the surrender at Appomattox, only to learn that he had lost more than the war. The family farm was gone, and so was the family.

It was perhaps the bitterest lesson of his life to learn that the North had no corner on greed and dishonor. And he had learned, too, that a wise man turns his back least on those he knows best. The rage that exploded in him then was more controlled now, but still there. He had burned the family farm to the ground, and buried those who had taken it from him. Since riding out of Georgia that bitter day, he had never looked back. But he hadn't forgotten.

Bradley, with all his pious posturing, was no better than a pickpocket. And, unlike a more forthright thief, he didn't even have the courage to do his thieving in the open. Instead, he hid behind the law. But what Slocum couldn't understand was why he should be a victim. What difference could it make to Barrett and Bradley what he did? But there was no doubt in his mind that this railroading was no accident. And to drag in another innocent man, who just happened to be a resident of the town, made it more curious still.

Bradley stared intently at Slocum, as if he were trying to read the younger man's mind. He found Slocum unsettling in a way he didn't quite undersand. He had been faced with other hard men, some, in one way or another, much harder than Slocum. But there was something about this man that he couldn't understand. He made a mental note to tell Barrett to keep a close eye on him.

Under Barrett's prodding, Slocum shuffled toward Bradley, then on past him and out through the rear door. He stared at the judge until it was no longer possible to see him. Outside, the heat was even more stifling than it had been an hour before. The sun was well above the horizon, and all traces of the night's rain were gone. Already, the soil had begun to crumble, and the hot breath of air off the desert to the south swirled small clouds of dust ahead of it, spiraling in short columns where it was trapped in corners.

A buckboard, its tailgate down, stood hitched to a pair of draft horses. Barrett dragged a well-worn stool from its place against the building and shoved it into position just under the rear of the wagon.

"Get in, and don't even think about giving me an argument," Barrett said, rapping Slocum on the hip with the twin barrels of the Remington.

The two steps of the stool were just low enough to allow a shackled man to reach them, a nicety of design that Slocum observed with an ironic smile. Turning his back to the wagon, he managed the first step. Reaching for the second, he received some unexpected assistance. Barrett stepped forward and used the muzzle of the Remington to shove him backward. Slocum landed hard on his tailbone, and twisted to the side to relieve the sudden stabbing pain that shot through his limbs.

"You son of a bitch," he snarled.

"Save it, cowboy. You ain't seen nothing yet." Barrett

turned smartly on his heel and disappeared back into the rear of the makeshift courtroom.

A moment later he was back, this time poking his Remington into Carter's kidneys. The young farmer glanced briefly at Slocum before turning his back to negotiate the steps of the stool. He too received some assistance from the Remington. His fall was broken somewhat by Slocum, who swung his legs to one side just in time to cushion Carter's spine.

Barrett rapped Slocum across the knees as he withdrew his legs, but Slocum just grinned at him.

"You won't be so feisty this time tomorrow, I can guarantee you that."

"We'll see, won't we?"

"Damn right we will." Barrett climbed up into the front of the wagon and waited for the second deputy.

Clyde Clemmons closed the tailgate, hauled himself up into the driver's seat, and turned to the wagon bed. "You fellers ready?" When neither Slocum nor Carter responded, he shrugged. Clemmons jerked the hand brake off and snapped the reins. Clucking to the horses, he urged them into a reasonable gait. The tightly sprung wagon jounced from side to side, and the two passengers in the rear, their hands cuffed behind them, had a rough time keeping themselves stable.

Barrett turned sideways and propped one booted foot on the seat. The shotgun dangled casually from one hand. Slocum eyed it thoughtfully. There was no chance of getting it from Barrett, but he was concerned that it might go off accidentally.

"You mind pointing that thing someplace else?" Slocum asked.

"What? This?" Barrett swung the muzzle toward Slocum, who was lying with his head right against the front wall of the wagon bed. The gun was inches above him, and he tried not to let Barrett sense his fear. "Don't worry

about this," Barrett laughed. "Your head gets blown off if
and when I'm ready. Not before."

"That's good to know, Barrett." Slocum turned his head
to the side and shifted his body slightly, bracing his shackled feet against the side of the wagon.

"You got sand, Slocum, I got to give you that." Barrett
laughed. "But you know what?" he asked, sweeping his
free hand in a broad arc, indicating the barren countryside,
"Around here, sand don't count for a whole lot."

Slocum turned his attention to Randy Carter, who
hadn't said a word since he climbed into the wagon.
Carter's eyes were closed, but his body was too rigid for
him to be sleeping. Slocum wanted to engage him in conversation, but there seemed little likelihood the young
farmer would respond.

Straight overhead, the sky was that overheated blue that
turns almost white under a hot sun. He stared up at the
incandescent air for several minutes, until the wagon
lurched into a gradual left turn. Suddenly the sun itself was
staring back at him. Its heat assaulted his skin immediately,
and he realized he hadn't had a drink since the night before. His clothes were soaked with perspiration, and the
smell of two sweating bodies seemed trapped in the shallow wagon bed, surrounding him like a thick gel.

As if Barrett had read his mind, the deputy grabbed a
canteen from under the wagon seat and twirled the cap
loose. Slocum watched him take a long pull on the water,
then offer it to Clemmons, who shook his head no.

"The prisoners might be thirsty, though."

"That right?" Barrett asked. "You thirsty, Slocum?"

Slocum nodded. "A bit."

Barrett started to lower the canteen, then, as if he had a
better idea, he raised it again. "Open wide," he said.

Tilting the canteen, he let a thin trickle of water spill
out. It was unsteady, with the wagon bouncing on the
rough road. "Catch it now, cowboy. We don't want to
waste it." The tiny silver stream dribbled over Slocum's

face, running into his nose. He managed to catch a few
drops on his outstretched tongue before Barrett righted the
canvas-covered container.

"That enough?" Barrett demanded. "Or are you still
thirsty?"

"You got no need to treat him like that, Clay."

"Clemmons, you got a need to mind your own business."

"Sheriff Millburn wouldn't like it."

"The sheriff is dead, Clyde, remember? The judge runs
Flat Creek now. You don't work for Millburn no more. You
work for the judge, just like everybody else who used to
work for Millburn. You'd best remember that. Besides, the
judge is a fair man, ain't he? Gave you a fair price for your
farm, didn't he?"

Clemmons was silent for a long minute. When he finally spoke, he said nothing about his farm. "That mean he
runs you too, Clay?" he asked.

"You know better'n that, Clyde. You surely do."

Clemmons shut up and concentrated on the horses. Slocum was intrigued by the exchange. He tossed it around for
the rest of the trip. He couldn't decide how it might be
useful, but there was something about it that warned him
not to forget it.

The wagon jerked to a halt, and Barrett jumped down.
Carter opened his eyes but still said nothing. Clemmons
kicked the brake on, looped the reins around the lever, and
jumped to the ground. Slocum watched him, visible from
the chin up, as he walked to the rear of the wagon. The
gate slammed down, and Barrett planted himself at one
corner of the wagon.

"All right boys, rise and shine."

Slocum sat up and hauled himself forward with his
shackled feet. When his legs dangled over the end of the
wagon, he dropped carefully to the ground. The impact
jarred his spine, and his head felt like it would split open.

Carter hauled himself forward in the same fashion.

When he dropped off the end of the wagon, he lost his balance and sprawled in the dust. He landed heavily. The wind had been knocked out of him, and he gasped for air. The raspy breathing, exaggerated by his thirst, sounded like a swarm of angry insects scratching at a screen.

Barrett poked him with the butt of the Remington. "No laying down on *this* job, partner. Get up."

When Carter was able to sit up, Clemmons reached down and gave him a hand. On his feet again, he shook himself like a wet dog to rid himself of the dust and sand.

"Don't worry about the dirt, Carter," Barrett advised him, "you'll get plenty dirty before your time is up. You can count on that."

Carter glared at the deputy, who walked away, tossing over his shoulder, "Keep an eye on them, Clemmons. I'll be right back."

Slocum watched Barrett depart, then turned his scrutiny on the prison. A tall palisade of rough lumber, topped by several strands of barbed wire, enclosed a compound nearly an acre in size. A barbed-wire gate, now open, gave access to the compound. Slocum noticed three rough wooden buildings, more like bunkhouses than anything else. They were arranged in a "U," with the open end toward him. In the center of the building that formed the bottom of the "U" a solid-looking wooden door, banded with a half-dozen steel straps, hung from heavy hinges. The door was windowless.

Two small windows on either side of the door were barred. A smaller building, of the same material but only half the length of the others, stood just inside the gate. Slocum guessed it was where the guards were quartered.

Off to the left, just outside the gate, a rail bumper stood between a set of railroad tracks that vanished into the flat, dry countryside. Two empty handcars sat on the end of the siding, just beyond the bumper. Across the compound, beyond the rear fence, Slocum noticed several tall mounds of railroad ties. Even as he spotted them, the heavy stench of fresh creosote reached his nostrils.

"So *this* is what it looks like." They were the first words Carter had spoken.

Slocum turned to face him. "You knew about this place?"

"Sort of. I mean, everybody has heard rumors, but nobody I know has been here. It's usually where the judge sends drifters. I guess I must be special, huh." He laughed bitterly.

"What the hell is it, anyway?"

"It's a work camp, Slocum. Free labor for Judge Bradley."

"What are you talking about?"

"The judge owns just about everything for fifty miles to the north. And what he doesn't own, he controls. But the land isn't worth much without a railroad. Nobody wants to build one, so the judge is building his own."

"With slave labor?"

"You're from Georgia, ain't you? You should know all about that, Slocum."

"You're telling me that we are going to spend the next ninety days building that bastard a railroad?"

"If we live that long, yeah, that's just what I'm telling you."

"Not on your life, Carter. No way."

"What do you propose to do about it?"

"I'll tell you exactly what I propose to do about it, I'm . . ." Barrett walked back through the gate, a tall man in a black coat right behind him.

"Welcome to hell, boys." Judge Bradley wasn't smiling.

Clay Barrett, standing behind the judge, had no such solemnity about him.

6

Barrett led the way to the building on the left. A rough plank boardwalk ran half the width of the barracks-like structure with the door at its center. Barrett grabbed a makeshift wooden handle and tugged the door open, then stepped aside for Slocum and Carter to enter. It was dark inside and even hotter than outside. The barred windows had no glass, but they were too small to compensate for the incredible heat of the sun beating on the plank and tarpaper roof.

A dozen bunks, fitted end to end, ran the length of one wall. They were bolted to the floor, and the heads of the bolts had been deformed by heavy blows. They were in to stay. The building was too narrow for anything else to be squeezed in. Under each bunk, a small footlocker, its metal fittings discolored with age, filled two-thirds of the space.

"It ain't pretty," Barrett said. "Is it?"

The new prisoners said nothing. Clemmons appeared in the doorway. "Clyde," Barrett snapped, "get them chains and cuffs off these bastards." He moved to one side, ac-

43

cepting Clemmons's shotgun before the deputy fished in his pocket for the keys. He undid Slocum's cuffs, then knelt to release the shackles. In an economy of effort, he hunched over to unlock the chains on Carter's ankles, then straightened up to remove the handcuffs.

Barrett handed the shotgun back, then sent Clemmons out of the barrack. When the deputy was gone, he turned to Slocum.

"The two bunks on the end are vacant. You could flip a coin for first pick. Course, you don't *have* coins, but you're big boys. You'll think of something. You'll find your uniforms in them lockers. One size fits all. Get changed. I'll be back in a half hour. You better be ready."

"Ready for what?" Slocum asked.

"Just be ready, that's all I'm gonna say." Barrett stomped across the wooden floor to the door and closed it behind him; the sound of a heavy bar dropping into place punctuated his departure.

Carter flopped down on the end bunk. Slocum took the other. The first thing he noticed was the smell. It was thick, the stench of ancient perspiration. It smelled as if the air in the barrack hadn't changed in a decade. Under the sweat, urine and other bodily secretions added grace notes of their own. The whole heady stew was overpowering.

"Stinks in here," Slocum said "I don't know about you, but I sure as hell am not going to spend ninety days in this cesspool."

"You got no choice," Carter whispered.

"All right, maybe I don't, but until I know that for sure, I'm gonna keep on looking for one."

"He'll kill you, you know. If you give him half a reason, he'll backshoot you. And there ain't nobody can stop him. And nobody will do a damn thing about it afterwards, either."

"You ready to tell me what's going on here?"

"What's the difference? Knowin' won't change things.

It'll just make you mad, make you careless. That happens, and they win."

"Looks like they're close to winning already. I don't see how knowing what I'm up against can make it any worse."

"What do you want to know?" Carter stood up and walked to the window while he waited for Slocum's first question. He leaned close to the opening and took a deep breath. He seemed to nod off, resting his hands on his folded arms. Then, as if awaking from a coma, he looked around the barrack, taking its measure with a single sweep of his eyes.

Carter pushed himself away from the window by extending his arms, then sat on his bunk. He bent down and tugged the footlocker from under the bunk. He opened the lid and pulled out his uniform. Faded denim shirt and jeans, both stenciled in white with the letters "CON" on front and back, the uniform was an amorphous-looking collection of rags.

"I wonder how many men have worn that thing," Slocum said.

"I don't know. Might as well add one more, though." Carter stood up and unbuttoned his own shirt, slipped it off, and tossed it into the trunk. He slipped the uniform shirt on, leaving it unbuttoned, then sat down and pulled off his boots. He changed his pants and tugged his boots back on, then sat back down with a sigh.

"Tell me everything you know about Clay Barrett," Slocum said. While he listened to Carter's answer, he changed into his own uniform, interrupting once or twice with requests for clarification.

When Carter was finished, Slocum nodded slowly, then asked, "And you knew all that when you tried to help me?"

"Yeah. I knew all that."

"Why'd you do it?"

"How could I not?"

"You must have been aware of the risk you were taking."

"No, I wasn't. Bradley's never sentenced anybody local to this prison. Only strangers. Footloose cowboys, hired hands drifting from job to job. Nobody with any roots in Flat Creek, or anyplace close."

"In other words, nobody likely to have somebody snooping around after him, nobody with family or friends to make a fuss."

"Or to get the territorial government involved," Carter added. He seemed to brighten at the thought. "Maybe that's our way out. Maybe Sissy can do something to get us out of here."

"I still don't see why you helped me. You hardly know me. Hell, we played cards for an hour or so. You never laid eyes on me before that."

"Look, Slocum, sometimes you get fed up with being pushed around. I guess I'd been feeling that way for a long time, but I never did anything about it. Maybe I forgot how. Maybe, when you called Barrett out after the poker game, you reminded me of something I used to know."

"What might that be?"

"That a man who won't stand up for himself can't expect anybody else to do it for him. As long as everybody walks around looking at their feet, they won't see what's going on right in front of their noses. It's time that changed."

"Maybe you're giving me too much credit."

"Maybe so. But I know one thing for damn sure. I ain't been giving myself half enough for too goddamn long. But that's over. I ain't going to be pushed no further. Hell, I came all the way across the country after the war. I didn't like the war, the killing, but I did it because it was my duty. I figure I paid my dues. I had enough of killing. But I guess the only way to prevent bloodshed is to be willing to risk it."

"Sounds nice, but we got to get out of here first."

"Then what? Where can I go? I bust out of here, they'll come after me, sure as hell. I put too much blood in what little land I got, Slocum. I ain't giving it up. Not now. I worked too hard for it."

"You said it yourself, though. The territorial governor can put a stop to it."

"Maybe. But politicians are all alike. You scratch one, they all bleed."

"Maybe, but until you think of something better, that's all we got."

The door banged open, and Barrett stood framed against the glaring blue-white sky. "Ready?"

"We're ready," Slocum said.

Barrett moved aside, and the two men stepped out into the open air. The sun was almost overhead, and their truncated shadows scurried ahead of them like strange desert animals. Barrett led the way to the small building just inside the gate. He held the door, indicating that the two men should enter.

Inside, seated at a small desk that had seen better days, Abel Bradley drummed his fingers on a stack of papers. Clyde Clemmons sat on a chair in one corner. Two other men, both armed with Colt revolvers and Springfield carbines, leaned against the wall behind Bradley.

"You gentlemen might as well make the best of your stay here," the judge began. "I don't mind telling you, I hate to see men forced into circumstances like these."

"That's not what I hear," Slocum said.

Bradley looked up sharply. His eyes narrowed, but his face was otherwise impassive. He seemed to be studying Slocum with a certain curiosity, the way an entomologist would scrutinize an example of a previously unknown species of insect. He leaned back in the chair, and it creaked in protest at the shifting weight.

"Is that so?" Bradley asked. "And just what *do* you hear, Mr. Slocum."

"You don't have to ask me that. You already know the answer."

"Indulge me, sir. Indulge me."

"Screw you, Your Honor. Or should I say 'Your Highness'? That's what you're doing, isn't it, playing king of the hill? You get away with murder because no—" A sudden piercing pain slashed through Slocum's shoulder. He grabbed his collarbone, and turned to see Barrett grinning at him.

"You got to have more respect for the law, Slocum. The judge ain't used to people mouthing off at him."

"I'll bet he's not. Maybe he ought to *get* used to it, though. I got a feeling it's going to become a habit."

"What do you mean?" The questioner was Bradley himself.

"Don't pay no attention to him, Judge. He's just talking."

"No, no, I want to hear. You know, Mr. Slocum, the Bible says that 'When the wicked man turneth away from his wickedness that he hath committed, and doeth that which is lawful and right, he shall save his soul alive.'"

"Maybe you ought to pay more attention to the Good Book, Judge, all of it, not just those parts that suit you. The Bible also says that 'The law is good, if a man use it lawfully.' Looks like to me, we got a mighty big 'if' staring at us here."

"You surprise me, sir. I wasn't aware that you were a man acquainted with the Scriptures."

"There's a lot about me that might surprise you."

"So I'm beginning to see, Mr. Slocum. Clay, show Mr. Slocum and Mr. Carter to their duties."

Slocum regretted his outburst. The last thing he needed was someone looking into his background. More than a few wanted posters concerning him were still in circulation. If Bradley turned one of them up, Slocum just might be looking at something worse than ninety days at hard labor, a whole lot worse. He'd have to bite his tongue from now on, and hope the judge came up empty on the inquiries he was almost certain to make.

Barrett led the way outside. With Clemmons riding shotgun, they walked to the gate and turned the corner. Following the stockade fence, they turned its corner. Ahead, Slocum saw the tail end of a low flatbed railcar. As they neared the rear fence, he heard loud voices and the dull thud of wood on wood.

Rounding the end of the rear fence, he saw the source of the noise. Two pairs of men, under the watchful eye of a pair of guards, were busily loading railroad ties onto the other end of the flatcar. Adjacent to the siding that held the flatcar, a second set of rails featured a small locomotive. As they approached, the engine rumbled. A power winch began to strain as it lifted a stack of rails. Four more men, like the others dressed in prison uniforms, were busy with the loading. One man operated the winch, two others guided the stack of rails toward the center of the flatcar, and the fourth stoked the fire in the engine's hotbox.

An additional guard, shotgun across his knees, sat on the rails that had already been loaded onto the flatcar. Looking at the laboring convicts, Slocum knew why the barrack stank of sweat. The men were soaked through, their faded denim darkened by the perspiration to such a degree that it might have been taken straight from a wash-tub.

Barrett told the two newcomers to wait for him, then walked over to the flatcar. He called up to the guard atop the rails, but Slocum couldn't hear what was said over the noise of the engine and the creaking winch. He walked back with a thoughtful expression on his face. Beckoning to one of the guards supervising the loading of the ties, he waited impatiently until the guard joined him.

Slocum looked up at the sky, and shaded his eyes with his hand as he spotted the sun. By its position in the sky, he estimated the time as a little past noon. He was starving, but knew better than to make an issue of it. If the men were fed, he would eat. If they weren't, asking for food would be asking for trouble.

Barrett walked off, turning once to look over his shoulder. The new guard approached them and directed them to form a third team for loading ties.

"Watch the others, and you'll figure it out pretty quick. And don't drop one of them things on your foot. You'll wish you hadn't, I can guarantee that. You'll be limping for the rest of your life." He backed away and resumed his position against the fence.

The men lifted the ties two at a time, one man at either end, and lugged them to the flatcar. Their legs bowed under the weight. They moved like ducks on land, the spread-legged waddle almost comical, if you ignored the massive weight they carried. Once the pair of ties was at the flatcar, the lead man strained to lift his end and thumped it down on the wooden bed of the flatcar.

Together the men shoved the ties all the way onto the car, then returned for another pair. When eight pairs were in place, the men climbed onto the car and moved the ties again, arranging them in crisscross stacks. Bending and lifting took a toll on their backs and legs. The stacks were nearly head high, and lifting the last few layers into place seemed to drain them of their energy.

"Listen," Slocum said to the guard, "why don't you rotate. Instead of having everybody doing everything, divide the work up, then switch teams once in a while. It would be easier."

The guard listened politely. When Slocum finished, he turned his head slightly and spat a thin stream of viscous tobacco juice that narrowly missed Slocum. Looking down at the dark, sticky glob alongside his foot, Slocum shook his head. Spitting again, the guard cleared his throat before answering.

"Listen, cowboy, this here is a prison. It ain't *supposed* to be easy. Now, unless you got any other dumb questions, why don't you and your partner there grab some of them ties and get to work?" He turned and moved down along the fence.

Slocum was about to follow him when he felt Carter's thick fingers digging into his arm.

"Forget it, Slocum. We're here for the duration. Just let it be."

7

Slocum lay on his bunk, his clothes soaked with sweat. He was too tired to move. Every joint in his body ached. His hands were sticky with creosote and blistered from constant contact with the rough wood. Several small tears in his skin still oozed blood where he had removed splinters. He closed his eyes and covered them with one arm. The rest of the men milled around in the narrow space between the bunks and the wall, except for Carter, who also sprawled on his own bunk.

Clemmons and two other guards entered the barrack carrying a stack of tin dishes, two pails, each sporting a dipper, and a few hunks of grainy cornbread. "Come and get it," Clemmons bellowed.

The men lined up in a ragged file. The tail end of the line was beside Slocum's bunk. The stench of sweat surrounded him, threatening to smother him. His stomach churned, but there was nothing in it to come up. He turned on his side and waited until the dry heaves passed.

The last man in line, a burly, bearded giant, nudged

Slocum with the toe of his boot. "You better get it while the gettin's good, partner. It ain't too good, and there ain't much of it, but if you want to keep your skin full, you better eat."

Slocum groaned. He looked up at the man and nodded, but he was too tired, and his throat too dry, to try to speak. The big man wore a sleeveless shirt, and Slocum noted his massive upper arms. They were a deep copper color and reminded Slocum of hams he'd cured and hung in the smokehouse back in Georgia. The very thought of home was like a rusty knife slipped in between his ribs. The thought of a good meal turned the knife a time or two. He thought he was going to choke.

"I'll get you something, if you want it."

"No thanks," Slocum croaked. He sat up on the bunk, waiting until the line moved forward a bit, then stood behind the friendly giant.

When he reached the head of the line, one of the guards slapped a dented tin dish into his hands then tossed a hunk of the cornbread into the dish. The bread was so stale, it rattled like a stone on the metal plate. The next guard dipped some pasty gruel and deposited it on the plate, where it slowly settled. The bread rattled across the tin and stuck to the gruel. The second dipper hoisted a quantity of thin, stringy meat that might have been beef, in a watery, brownish gravy. The smell of the meat almost hid the pervasive sweat smell. The guard indicated the corner, where a bucket of warm water, a thin skin of a faintly greenish cast covering its surface, stood beside a stack of handleless tin cups.

"All right, chow down. We'll be back in twenty minutes for the empties," Clemmons announced. He led the way out of the barrack, and the heavy bar slammed into place.

Slocum walked back to his bunk and sat down, balancing the plate on his closed knees. There were no utensils, and he watched the others transport the sticky gruel from plate to mouth with practiced ease, using the rocklike bread as a spoon. The meat was another matter. Using their fingers, the men grabbed it two or three strips at a time and shoveled it down.

Slocum tasted the gruel and nearly gagged. Its bitter, gluey taste clung to the inside of his mouth, and he washed it down with a swallow of the warm water. The meat by now was awash in the gruel, and he picked a strip out of the mess and wiped the gruel off by stripping the stringy meat between two closed fingers. It still tasted of the glutinous paste, and it smelled like it had been around awhile, but at least it was chewable. He ate the meat and left the rest, downing the remains of his water with a single gulp.

Carter was already asleep, and Slocum wasn't sure how long it would be before he joined the young farmer, whether he wanted to or not. Clemmons was back right on time. He and his crew collected the plates and cups, leaving the pail of water and a clean dipper. Slocum lay down and tugged a thin blanket up over his chest. He was asleep almost instantly.

When he awoke, it was nearly dawn. Pale gray showed through the small windows. A rustle in the far corner caught his ear. He sat up soundlessly, trying to see into the shadows. The sound of water running into a pool echoed off the wooden walls, and Slocum realized someone was using the latrine bucket. He lay back on the bunk, still bone weary but wide awake. There was no point in trying to get back to sleep. Sunup was less than an hour away, and he knew from conversation with one of the convicts the previous afternoon that they would be up and out early.

While he lay there, he considered his options. They were few, and none was attractive. He could grit his teeth and try to tough it out. He might be able to take the harassment, but he was more than half convinced that Carter was right. Barrett had it in for him, for some reason that went way beyond the fight in the bar. Whether Barrett was a killer or not was a question he could only answer through experience. If the answer was yes, it would be too late. If it was no, that still left eighty-nine days of brutal labor, and summer was just ahead. The temperature would rise another twenty or thirty degrees. He could endure it, but he saw no reason to have to. So, on balance, toughing it out was unacceptable.

On the other hand, he could try to escape. That, at first blush, seemed more attractive. But it was far less realistic. Assuming he managed to get away, how far could he expect to get? Unarmed, horseless, and without water, his chances in the high desert were minimal. Water he could get. A gun he might be able to manage. But a horse was next to impossible. Without a horse, he would be hunted down in a matter of hours, with or without water and a gun. And if, by some fluke, he managed to avoid capture, there was no place to go without stopping first at Flat Creek. That, of course, was the first place they'd look. So escape was more hazardous than toughing it out.

There was only one other option, but he didn't think it had much chance either. It had been a long time since anyone had seen a miracle. That made escape, as unlikely as it was, the only realistic alternative.

While he debated with himself, he realized that he would need more information. If he were to try to escape, he'd need to know a hell of a lot more about the surrounding terrain than he knew now. That meant either pumping someone who knew, or getting someone to go along with him. Carter knew the area, so he was a candidate, but he had shown little inclination to talk since they had arrived. Whether he was ready for something even more demanding was uncertain.

He resolved to use the morning to gather as much information as he could. It wouldn't pay to move too soon. If he caught them by surprise, he might have a chance, but only if they didn't have a surprise of their own waiting for him. He lay back and watched the changing color of the light. The deep gray turned to pale gray, then suddenly to blood red. The sun had just climbed above the horizon, and he could see it in his mind's eye. He'd always wondered why the rising and setting sun seemed so gigantic compared to its midday size, and why it seemed so flat, as if it were being squeezed into the ground by some unseen hand.

As the red turned to orange, the other convicts started to stir. More accustomed to the prison's schedule, their bodies had internalized the institutional clock, just as he had the Army clock during the war. It was probably some primitive instinct to avoid conflict with a system that enabled men to adapt so easily.

The first one up was the big man with the beard. He had tried to be helpful the night before. He might be a good source to tap for information. The big man got up and walked to the latrine corner. Slocum waited until he had finished, then walked to the window just opposite the big man's bunk.

Slocum glanced at the sun, then turned to the big man. He stuck out his hand, and the bear grasped it firmly. "The name's Slocum. I was too damn tired to thank you last night."

"Carly Duncan. And don't mention it. And don't fret the agony. You get used to it after a while. A man can get used to anything, I guess, if he has too."

"I hope I don't get used to *this*." Slocum smiled.

"How long you in for?" Duncan asked.

"Ninety days. Eighty-nine now."

"Don't count on it."

"What do you mean?"

"You see any calendars here? Any clocks?"

Slocum was puzzled. "I don't understand," he said.

"I got thirty days, myself. That was nearly two months ago. The judge seems to own everything, including time. He can't stop the sun from risin' and settin', but that don't mean he has to count."

Slocum shook his head. "I don't believe it."

"You'd better. And if you got ninety, you better plan for

a long, long haul, Slocum. I had to do ninety, I'd be fig-
gerin' a way out, I was you."

"Don't think I'm not. I'd like to talk to you later, if you
don't mind."

"Talk's easy to come by. Just don't let them see you. We
get out on the line, they'll be all over your ass. But we get
a lunch break. Maybe then."

"Thanks."

"But Slocum . . ." He paused for a moment before con-
tinuing. "You want help, you're talkin' to the wrong guy.
I'll tell you what I know, but that's all. Thirty days might
be a little longer than usual around here. But I still figger I
can walk away a free man. Beats ridin' away a dead one."

Slocum nodded. He wanted to ask a few more questions, but before he could decide how to frame them, he
heard the grating of the bar on the door. Clemmons stepped
in, a triangle in one hand. With the other he rattled the
triangle with a railroad spike. The racket woke Carter and
one other man who was still sleeping.

"Rise and shine, boys, rise and shine. We got work to
do."

Clemmons left, and the men scrambled to get dressed.
Across the compound, just audible above the din in the
barrack, Slocum heard Clemmons repeat his triangle routine twice. The men tumbled out in the bright sunlight and
assumed a ragged double file. Barrett strode across the
yard, a carbine slung over his shoulder. He took a quick
head count, then walked back across to count the other two
groups.

Four guards appeared to herd the men through the front
gate. Slocum watched as the men in front climbed onto the
flatcar, grabbing handholds where they could. The small
engine had already been switched and sat in front of the
flatcar, its stack nervously puffing gray smoke. When the
men had all clambered onto the flatcar, Slocum counted
heads. Thirty-three, not counting the guards. Six more

prisoners manned three handcars, each carrying two guards, each armed with a shotgun or a carbine, as well as a sidearm. Six more guards rode in the engine. That made twelve guards for thirty-nine men. Better than three-to-one odds. If you ignored the weapons.

But Slocum knew better than that.

The train pulled out, the men clinging to whatever came to hand to avoid being shaken loose. The stacks of ties, lashed with heavy rope, creaked and groaned. The rails, also lashed down, squealed as metal grated against metal as the car rocked from side to side. As the engine swung into a gentle curve, Slocum had the sensation of falling. The ties beneath him shifted, and one slipped free, rattling down the stack and bouncing off the car altogether. The others held fast, and Slocum shifted his weight, trying to get to a more secure position.

Carly Duncan sat to Slocum's right and a bit below. Slocum reached out with a boot and tapped him on the rump. Duncan turned to look at him, but scowled to indicate it was not a good idea to talk. Slocum nodded that he understood, and settled down to wait out the ride. The sun was already climbing into the sky, and the wood of the ties felt warm beneath his hands.

Bright light glinted from the gleaming ends of the rails themselves. They were brand-new, and the curved, shiny top surface was smooth and unmarked. The reflected glare was painful to look at, and Slocum closed his eyes. He listened to the clack of the wheels on the rails beneath him. Its rhythm was hypnotic. Nodding in time to the clatter, Slocum felt himself drifting. He tried to focus his mind on the problem of escape, but all he could think about was the odds. He knew far too little to take a chance. All he could do was hope that, as he learned more about the habits of the guards, the odds would shift a little in his favor.

It would help if he could get to talk to a few of the men from the other two barracks. He couldn't believe that no one else wanted to escape, no matter what the risks. His situation was unique, perhaps, because he had had the run-in with Barrett, and pride was an issue when it came to Slocum. On the other hand, it was beginning to strike home that he had been suckered.

Barrett and Bradley had somehow used Karen Alston to set him up. It made no difference that it was John Slocum. In fact, they couldn't have cared less. But they wanted cheap labor, and any warm body would do. Unfortunately, he had taken the same attitude when he agreed to go to bed with Karen Alston. But he was baffled by the woman's willingness to perjure herself, and let herself be doubly used.

On the other hand, the bruises on her face were real. Barrett had beaten her severely, and yet she had cooperated with the frame. That could only mean one thing—whatever Barrett and/or Bradley could do to her was more frightening than the thought of what an innocent man might do once he served his time. Slocum knew that he would see her again. And he didn't doubt that most men in his position would go looking for her at the first opportunity. She had to know that.

But if she did know it, and still went along with Barrett, then Barrett had some sort of hold over her, something that mattered to her more than anything else in the world. If only he could discover what that hold might be, then perhaps he might be able to understand why she had done what she had done. He wasn't prepared to forget, nor even to forgive, but understanding went a long way. If he could understand, then he might be able to walk away.

The train started to slow down, its brakes squealing in protest. As Slocum jumped down from the flatcar, he looked off into the vastness of the desert. Even at this altitude, it was overwhelmingly arid. The mountains in the northern distance seemed closer than they were. Slocum knew, from painful experience, that measurement had no meaning in the desert. The high peaks, still covered with snow, might as well be on the moon.

Watching the sunlight glitter on the ice and snow, he thought it must be what heaven looked like from the gates of hell.

8

Slocum got himself assigned to the same team as Carly Duncan. They worked on laying ties. One by one, they unloaded the heavy wood and staggered up the line to drop it in place. Then, dropping to their knees, they pushed and shoved, wiggling the ties until they were properly spaced. Then it was back to the flatcar for another pair.

In the meanwhile, a second team of men spiked the heavy metal plates that held the rails in place. It was an efficient use of manpower, but it meant an additional obstacle for Slocum and Duncan as they staggered from the flatcar. Each time, they had to maneuver around the spikers with their heavy load.

When enough ties had been laid, the rails were lowered into position. A small manual crane on the tail of the flatcar dropped each rail to a point just above the ties, where two men could guide it into place. Each one dropped with a clank onto the plates, then it was spiked home by teams of men wielding heavy sledgehammers. The incessant slam of the sledges and the knell-like toll of metal on metal gave

Slocum a splitting headache. It was impossible to think clearly with the racket, so he used the time to observe.

The guards seemed rather relaxed about their responsibilities, as if they were convinced that the desert itself was enough of a deterrent. They gathered in small knots, talking among themselves. Once in a while one of them would split off from his group and drift along the railbed, barking at the prisoners, but it seemed to be a pro forma gesture rather than one full of genuine hostility. There were three exceptions, however.

Two of the guards kept to themselves, preferring neither to socialize with their fellows nor to fraternize with the convicts. One of them, a small, barrel-shaped man, sported an angry scar that ran from his left ear to the tip of his stubby chin. According to Carly Duncan, his name was James Allen, and no one, even the other guards, seemed to know much more about him than that.

Allen sported a weathered black bullwhip hung in tight coils over the butt of his Colt revolver. For most of the guards, their work was just that, a job. It put money in their pockets. Like most workers, they didn't want to do any more than was necessary to ensure the continued receipt of a paycheck. They seemed to operate on the theory that without prisoners, there'd be no need for guards. With that in mind, they tended to be indifferent, as long as nobody gave them a hard time.

But Allen, according to Duncan, was a breed apart. Duncan had seen him beat a man to death with the whip. One of the prisoners, a Mexican who had virtually no English, had wandered away from the railbed to take a piss. He had either failed to hear or misunderstood Allen's command to halt. The barrel-shaped guard had fired a shot in the air and then, when the Mexican had stopped, taken after him with the whip. He continued to lash out at the man, who had fallen to the ground with his shirt already in tatters, and the skin of his back and shoulders nearly flayed.

The other guards had tried to drag Allen away, but he continued to flail away with the whip, cracking it again and again across the now unconscious Mexican's prostrate body, even as the other guards hauled him physically away. Barrett, when the other guards demanded that he intervene, had simply stood to one side and laughed.

"That's when I decided to watch my step, and to stay away from anybody who wouldn't watch his," Duncan said. The smile on his face was hard-edged and bitter.

"There was no need to do that man like that, Slocum. I swear to God, I never saw anything like it. The Mex looked like a piece of raw steak."

"What happened to him?" Slocum asked.

Duncan tilted his head out into the desert. "Out there. I expect the buzzards got him."

"They didn't even bury the poor bastard?"

"Unh-unh. Barrett wouldn't let them. Said it would be a nice little object lesson for us."

"And you don't want to do anything about it?"

"What the hell can I do? What can any of us do? They got the whip hand, so to speak. Slocum, you got to realize, they can blow your damn head off and there ain't a thing anybody can do about it. We're convicts, we're scum, the way folks look at it. They can get away with murder, and have."

"I'll be damned if I'll let them treat me like that," Slocum whispered. "Or anybody else, as long as I can do something about it."

"That's damn noble of you, Slocum. But the key words are as long as you can do anything about it. You can't do shit. The sooner you get that through your head, the more likely you are to get out of here alive."

"What about the other loner, the one hangs by himself all the time."

"Hell, he's even scarier than Allen. Some sort of Bible nut. Don't matter what you say to him, he throws some Scripture back at you. And he's got these eyes, like two small coals. Seems like you can look through his face all the way to hell. He seems harmless, but it wouldn't surprise me if he went out the back of the barn someday. If he blows, I got a feeling he's not going out alone. Stay out of his way, though, and you'll be okay."

"Barrett, you don't have to tell me that. I've seen enough of him, and of his kind. There's no surprise there."

"So? You seem to be leading up to something. What is it?"

"Everybody here feel the same way you do?"

"About what?"

"About everything. Everybody willing to put his time in?"

"Look, I don't know what you're getting at, but if it's what I think it is, leave me the hell alone."

"Come on, Duncan, you've been here long enough to know what's what. You must know if anybody's planning to get out."

"I don't, and if I did, I don't know you from a hole in the ground. You think I'd tell you about something like that, you must be stupid or crazy. Probably both."

"Look, I'm not asking for any names. But if you *do* know somebody, tell him to talk to me. Let him make up his own mind. But I'll tell you one thing, I'm not staying here one day longer than I have to. I'd like some help, but if I can't get any, I'm gonna do it myself. You said yourself that Barrett was a backshooter. The longer I wait, the better his chances are. I've got to move."

"What about your buddy, Carter. Why not him?"

"I don't know. I just don't think he wants to try it. He hasn't said two words since he got here."

"That's 'cause he's smart. Not like some hot-shot cowboys I know."

"Think what you want. But I'll tell you one thing. If I do get out, I'm coming back."

Duncan grunted noncommittally, then turned to his work, as if to tell Slocum he was through talking. The sun was merciless, and Slocum's shirt and jeans were soaked through. Lugging the ties from the front end of the flatcar was slowly grinding him down. He kept watching the sun, hoping he could hold out until break time.

From time to time, one of the guards came around with a pail of water, and Slocum stood panting beside the railroad car, craning his neck to find the water carrier. He felt a tap on his shoulder, and turned to see Barrett grinning at him.

"What's the matter, cowboy? Too tough for you out here? You should have thought about that before you got so smart in the hotel."

Slocum ignored him, hoping Barrett would go away, but the deputy had his claws dug in, and he wasn't going to leave until he ripped a little flesh. "You know, Slocum, I've seen dozens of hardcases like you. They're two bits a bushel. And I'll tell you another thing. Not one of them wasn't sorry he was such a bigmouth by the time he left here. I got a feeling you ain't gonna be no different."

Slocum turned away. He reached for his end of the next ties, but Barrett wasn't ready to leave him alone. He grabbed Slocum by the arm and spun him around. Slocum clenched his fists involuntarily, and Barrett laughed.

"Go ahead, you sonofabitch, hit me. It'll be the last thing you ever do." As if to emphasize his point, Barrett jabbed the muzzle of his shotgun into Slocum's belly. "You ever seen a man been gut-shot, Slocum? It ain't a pretty sight. And he's a long time dyin'. So go ahead, just give me an excuse." Barrett poked the gun deeper into Slocum's midsection, the hard metal scraping at the lower edge of his rib cage.

Slocum bit his tongue. He knew what Barrett was trying to do, and he refused to give him the satisfaction. He turned away again, and this time Barrett let him go.

Duncan called across the flatcar, "You finally ready?"

"All set," Slocum grunted as he half shoved and half lifted the heavy wood and crab-walked to the end of the car. Stepping toward Duncan, he propped the ties on his shoulder and took the lead. At six inches taller, Duncan had a mechanical advantage, and the downward slope of the tie placed a disproportionate share of the weight of each load on Slocum's shoulders. He was aware of the disparity, but he was convinced that Duncan was the key to his escape. If he had to hoist more than his share until he got what he wanted, that was all right.

They dropped the pair of ties, and Slocum knelt to bully the top one off and rolled it forward to its proper position. Duncan aligned the second tie, then got to his feet. "It's about lunchtime," he said. A second later, two blasts on the engine's horn confirmed his guess.

The prisoners converged on the engine, where the meager ration of cornbread and water would be allocated. Slocum looked for Randolph Carter, but the young farmer seemed to be avoiding him. He finally spotted him in a small group of men toward the front of the engine. He waved, but Carter failed to return the gesture.

Dropping down with a groan, Slocum propped his back against one wheel of the flatcar, ducking back out of the sun. When the mess bucket arrived, he took a mouthful of the water, using the dipper to part the thin greenish scum on the surface and swirling the water in his mouth a few times. When the thick, pasty taste of his thirst was gone, he spat the water into the dirt beside him and closed his eyes. Hunger was hard to take, but the rocklike bread was harder still.

After a few minutes he sensed a shadow in front of him, and he opened his eyes slowly to stare into the pendulous gut of another convict. The man turned and lowered himself onto the ground to Slocum's right.

Speaking in a whisper out of the side of his mouth, the man said, "Don't look at me. And don't say nothing. Just listen."

Slocum glanced at him carefully, but didn't recognize

the face. Whoever the man was, he wasn't in Slocum's barrack.

"Word has it you don't like it here much. I don't either, but it ain't gonna be easy. You willing to put your ass on the line?"

Slocum grunted assent.

"Okay. Here it is, then. After lunch, get on the spiking crew. Ask for Jack Hardy, tell him you're taking his place. Duncan already told him to expect you. Two o'clock, we'll be out of ties. They'll take the flatcar back to the camp for more. The guard detachment will be cut in half. That's when we make our move. You got a weapon?"

Slocum shook his head.

"That don't help none, but we'll have to make do. There's three of us, counting you. There should be two guards with the spiking crew. The others will be scattered around. I got horses coming, but we got to move like hell to get some ground behind us. Watch me, and stay close to one of the guards. I'll take care of the other one. When I drop my hammer, you make your move. And whatever you do, get his guns. You have to shoot, shoot to kill. Any questions?"

"None," Slocum whispered.

The man stood up and walked away, his nonchalance almost perfect. Despite the gut, he was an imposing figure. Slocum put his height at six foot three or so. Even from behind, the thick forearms were impressive. Slocum had no idea who the man was, but if you were going to break out of jail with strangers, it wouldn't hurt to have somebody that size on your side.

Slocum maneuvered his way onto the spiking crew as he had been told. As he began the afternoon's work, he felt the hair on his neck standing on end. The tension was getting to him. Part of him was convinced he was being set up. But he wanted out, and there was no such thing as a risk-free jailbreak.

The guards started to relax as the work gangs fell into

their rhythm. Slocum and the big man, whom someone called Martin, were at the leading end of the rail line, driving spikes as fast as the ties and plates were laid. They would take a breather as the rails were lowered into place, then work their way forward a second time, securing the rails with a second set of spikes. The big hammer felt good in his hands. He poured his energy into the work, and it helped to relax him.

Martin seemed to be waiting for something. From time to time he lifted his head to stare out over the desert. The glances were quick, but Martin was clearly getting impatient. After an hour, Slocum found himself wondering whether the whole thing was a false alarm. He tried to think of an excuse to approach Martin without attracting attention.

When they finished spiking the latest pair of rails, Slocum stepped across the roadbed and fell into line behind Martin. "You sure you got the right day?" he asked.

Martin turned, and the look on his face was enough to convince Slocum to hold his questions. They leaned against the flatcar, and Martin looked out over the desert again, this time taking a more leisurely survey.

"Fuck it, I can't take this no more," Martin hissed. "Let's do it." He tugged a hand-rolled cigarette from his shirt and approached the furthest guard, who was standing with his back to the flatcar at the railhead. Slocum sidled along after him, glancing around to spot the third man. He saw nothing out of the ordinary, and turned his attention to the other guard.

"You got a match, Scotty?" Martin asked.

The guard scowled, but reached into his own shirt pocket. Martin kicked him in the balls and drove a thick fist into Scotty's jaw, knocking him to the ground.

Slocum leaped on the second guard, snaking a forearm around his neck and under his chin. He squeezed hard, and the guard gasped for air.

"Break his goddamn neck," Martin hissed. He bent to

retrieve Scotty's weapons. He tucked the guard's revolver into his belt and slugged the prostrate man with the butt of his own shotgun.

"Where's the third man?" Slocum asked.

"Fuck him," Martin said.

"How the hell are we going to pull this off?" Slocum asked. It was too late to back out, but he cursed himself for hooking up with the big man.

He heard hoofbeats, and turned to see a single rider, trailing three saddled horses, approaching at full gallop. The other guards heard the commotion but seemed uncertain what to do. The horses skidded to a halt. Martin climbed into the saddle of one horse and Slocum mounted a second. They turned the third horse loose, and the three men headed out into the desert. The guards finally realized what was happening and started firing their weapons.

Slocum turned to see Martin's horse stumble. The animal tried to stand, but it had broken a leg. Slocum spun his horse in a tight turn, but Martin waved him back. The big man struggled to get out from under the fallen horse. "Get out of here," he shouted, waving his arms wildly.

Realizing Martin was down, the guards had begun to run across the slippery sand. Martin yanked the revolver from his belt and fired until it was empty. Thick clouds of black smoke swirled around him, shining like ebony in the brilliant sun. The guards hesitated until Martin stopped firing, then charged forward again as he raised the shotgun.

He held on as long as he could. The double-barreled Remington wasn't accurate at long range, and the guards knew it. When he realized they were going to sit outside his accuracy range, he let go with both shots, timing them carefully, hesitating before each, trying to buy as much of a head start for the others as he could.

Slugs whistled around Slocum's head, and he kicked the horse to go still faster. He kept watching, and saw Barrett, leading the pack, reach Martin, who now stood with his hands in the air. A slug slammed into Slocum's horse, and the animal broke stride for a second, nearly stumbled, then settled into a limping gait. High on the horse's left flank, twin streams of blood marked the entry and exit wounds. The blood flowed heavily, and Slocum knew it was only a matter of time before the horse cashed it in.

The third rider, whose horse was unharmed, was rapidly widening the gap between himself and Slocum. He turned once and waved his hat, as if to urge Slocum on.

As he stared back at the diminishing figures behind him, he saw Barrett raise his shotgun and stab it toward Martin, muzzle first. The big prisoner doubled over as Barrett stepped back. Still pointing the shotgun at the captured man, Barrett moved back a step further. Slocum thought he was issuing orders for shackles or handcuffs when he saw a bright flash and a dark halo. Martin fell to the ground.

When the sound first reached him, Slocum was puzzled. By the time he realized it was a shotgun a few moments later, Martin was already dead.

9

Slocum hunkered down into the brush. From the ridge, he could see the search team methodically working its way in a crisscross pattern across the valley floor. His horse was no longer even a speck on the valley floor. A circle of buzzards overhead had long since descended to commence their work.

His throat was parched. Scratches on his arms and legs burned as if they were on fire. Far behind him, he could see the Mazatzal Mountains, but there was no chance he could make it on foot, not with a dozen men on horseback hard on his trail.

Losing them would be his best bet. He had done his best to conceal his tracks, but he knew he had been only partially successful. And he had to cover nearly a hundred miles of high desert to reach Prescott. The country between was ripped and slashed by ragged valleys, littered with huge mesas to be avoided, and sliced by dry washes. Every mile would cost him two or three. The loose, rocky scree on the slopes of every valley made footing treacherous.

The mountains would be a picnic compared to it. And above all else, there was the sun.

On its downward slide now, it was still scorching. And when it set, if he lasted that long, he would have no light but the moon and the stars. Slocum knew enough about the desert to know that some of its more dangerous inhabitants moved mostly at night. But he had been a gambler all his life. And the odds of making it to Prescott were a hell of a lot better, bad as they were, than his chances of leaving Flat Creek alive if they caught him now.

He had seen what happened to Martin. Cold blood was too tame a term to describe how Barrett had shot him.

Every breath rasped in his throat like sandpaper. There was water here, he knew, in the cactus all around him, but their skins were tough and the spines too sharp. He had nothing to rip them open. If he could find a rock, something to get through the plants' defenses, he could get a little moisture to relieve his thirst. Getting to his feet, he backed away from the crest of the ridge, crouching to keep his profile low.

He had only two choices. He could stay on the ridge, just below the line, and move east or west. The traveling would be easier that way, but he wouldn't be getting any closer to Prescott. Or he could hazard the long, precipitous descent down the face of the ridge to the valley floor. It was Hobson's choice. Slocum sighed, feeling his throat close against the dehydrating rush of air.

A patch of green across the valley floor caught his eye, and he thought it might be a water hole. That made up his mind. Leaning backward to control his descent, he stepped off the ridge into the loose soil and started down. The men on his trail were too far away for him to hear anything but a gunshot. He dug his heels into the scree with every step, testing his footing. Slowly, he picked his way through the stubborn cactus that seemed to grow out of the very stones. Cholla and prickly pear, saguaro and barrel, and a hundred varieties he'd never seen before, each fighting for its own grip on the slope.

As he settled into a rhythm, he allowed himself a controlled slide, each step carrying him several feet down the gritty slope. He fought the urge to increase his speed, knowing that if he lost his balance, he wouldn't be able to stop himself. The boulders strewn across the face of the slope would crush his skull. A collision with a cactus could puncture him in a hundred places. The spines on some of the larger plants were six or eight inches long, and razor sharp. If he hit one of them at any speed, he'd be skewered like meat on a spit.

As he stepped and slid, stepped and slid, Slocum kept his eye on his goal. The dark green patch looked more promising as he came closer. He still had three thousand yards to cover, but his spirits had already begun to rise. Water. It was impossible to describe how sacred a fluid it could be, how precious, until you'd spent half a day under the crushing weight of the southwestern sun.

In his haste, he kicked over a small rock lodged in the sand, and an angry tarantula leapt out of the hole he'd uncovered. He knew they weren't as bad as their reputations, and he knew that nothing could be as bad as the hairy spider looked, but it's one thing to know it, and another to act on that knowledge. The sudden movement in the dead landscape startled Slocum. He twisted to one side as the arachnid flashed past him.

His left foot hit another rock, the heel slipping to one side. His legs splayed, and he lost his balance. Slocum threw his weight backward, landing on his back and shoulders. Fighting to keep control, he felt himself begin to slide.

His shirt hiked up, and the sand and gravel began to scrape away the bare skin of his back. He kept his legs raised to use their weight as a kind of tiller. A sturdy saguaro, nearly twenty feet tall, was dead ahead. Bracing himself for the impact, Slocum brought his feet together and slammed them into the base of the huge cactus. His spine felt as if it had been squeezed in a vise. But he stopped moving.

The crash knocked the air from his lungs, and he gasped painfully. His eyes were closed, and bright flashes, like shooting stars, stabbed off in every direction. Slowly regaining his composure, Slocum forced himself to breathe deeply, ignoring the rawness in his throat. He lay still for several minutes, his eyes canted back up the slope toward the crest of the ridge. He half expected to see a horse and rider appear miragelike on the shimmering crest.

Forcing himself to sit up, he searched the valley floor, still several hundred yards away; it was another thousand to the clump of thick green. There was no sign of movement. Scrambling to his feet, he resumed the descent. This time he moved more cautiously. He had been lucky once. But luck, as he well knew, was an addiction. As with any addiction, the demand was always greater than the supply.

He had seen men after the war, their bodies—and worse—their minds, so dependent on morphine they were no good without and worthless with it. The new drug, and the newly invented hypodermic, were supposed to be a cure-all, allowing wounded men to cope with the pain of injury and surgery. Instead, they had become a new affliction. He sometimes wondered whether luck was his morphine, and whether one day he would run out. It had been a long time since he'd felt so close to the end of his ration.

There was only one way to find out if this was his last hurrah.

The slope began to flatten out as he neared the valley floor, and the going got easier. The cactus was thicker, but he had more control over his descent. He wanted to run but knew he didn't have the strength. His energy was almost gone as it was. If he went flat out, and he was wrong about the water, he would be a dead man within a few hours.

Already, hatless under the blistering sun, he couldn't even be sure his eyes weren't playing tricks on him. Slocum knew that men see what they wanted to see more easily than they see what's in front of them. As he reached the floor of the valley, he slowed again. A twisted Joshua tree lay like a lone sentinel twenty yards ahead. Its sparse leaves and gnarled branches wouldn't give him much shade, but at least he could lean against its trunk and catch his breath.

He stumbled toward the tree and fell at its base, resting his cheek against the rough bark. The sand beneath him was hot, and he could feel it baking him as he lay there. His breath was ragged, and small clouds of dust danced around his face with each explosive gasp. His legs were made of India rubber. Turning on his back, he snaked around the tree until the shadow of its trunk fell across his face.

Slocum looked up at the incandescent sky with eyes that were nearly sightless. High above him, in broad, lazy circles, the buzzards were beginning to gather. He raised a fist to shake it at the birds.

"You bastards. You fucking bastards, not yet. I'm not dead yet."

He closed his eyes for a long moment. When he opened them, a black speck was dropping toward him like a stone. It seemed to pick up speed as it fell. His vision was blurred, and he wiped a sunburned hand across his eyes. The black speck was larger now, and falling even faster. Suddenly broad wings flared out as the bird began to brake. It was an eagle, and its great wings must have been four feet across. The gnarled talons, like two bony fists, were curled up against the bird's body. Slocum thought for a minute the bird was after him, but it shot past and struck at something twenty yards away. He turned on his stomach in time to see the eagle clutch at a scurrying lizard.

With a terrifying cry, the bird began to beat its wings, and, never quite touching the earth, it lifted away, the struggling lizard suddenly limp in the razor-sharp talons. The lizard's tail twitched twice and then went still, trailing out behind the bird and its prey like a slender reed bending in the current.

Slocum envied the bird.

He climbed to his feet, determined to reach the water hole. His legs threatened to buckle beneath him, but he pressed on. His knees were made of jelly. Every step made his boots heavier, and for one crazy second he thought about taking them off and leaving them behind.

He could see the green ahead of him, a few cottonwood trees taller and greener than anything he could see for miles in any direction. There had to be water. He felt his heart racing, every beat threatening to shatter his ribs. When he closed to within two hundred yards, he forced himself to stop. It wouldn't do to make a stupid mistake now.

He watched the tree line for a couple of minutes, squeezing his eyes to slits, trying to force them to focus clearly. It was a losing battle. He was too thirsty, too tired. The unrelenting heat had him on the verge of delirium. He pressed a hand to his forehead, and his skull felt like a hot rock. The skin was dry, like old parchment, and his brow had begun to swell. He had all the signs of sunstroke, and possibly sun poisoning.

At this point, Slocum realized, he needed the shade as much as he needed the water. He tried to estimate how far he'd come, and knew it couldn't be as far as it seemed. He wondered, too, why the guards chasing him had seemed content to take their time. Maybe, he thought, they were counting on the sun to kill him. It made no difference to them whether they brought him back alive, or kicked sand over his corpse and left him for the scavengers. All they really wanted to know was where he was.

Dropping to a crouch, he ducked from cactus to cactus, using whatever cover the arid terrain offered him. The closer he came to the tree line, the faster he moved, as if the water drew him like some powerful magnet. He knew he couldn't slow up even if he wanted to.

The small stand of trees was nothing much. Slocum did

a rough count as he approached. There couldn't have been more than twenty trees, if that. There was undergrowth, but not much of that either. Something, the wind, birds, had dropped a few seeds, and there had been enough water to get things started. From that point on, it was a constant struggle against the heat and the sun. The green was holding its own, but just barely.

Slocum stepped into the underbrush, sweeping it aside with one arm. The rough bark and a few thorns scratched at his sunburned skin. They were minor irritants. Passing the first couple of trees, he started to run, as fast as the scraggly brush would allow. He could smell the water. His nostrils flared, and he had begun to pant like a stray dog on a hot afternoon.

A few small birds chirped in the trees overhead, and Slocum almost smiled. It was like suddenly being returned to the real world after a nightmare. Things were almost normal here. It was small, but it would save his life. At least for the moment.

And then, like a mysterious jewel materializing out of thin air, came the water itself. Not deep, and not all that clean, a small spring-fed pond, no more than fifteen feet across and thirty feet long, if that, lay in a shallow depression, surrounded by trees on all sides. A few boulders were scattered through the brush on the far side. Slocum dropped to his knees. He laid the shotgun aside and pulled the revolver out of his belt. Bending from the waist, he scooped great handfuls of the tepid water to cool his skin. He ducked his head into the pond and felt the heat begin to drain from his scalp and forehead.

Greedily, he drank great gulps of water. Then, realizing how sick it could make him, he stopped. There was plenty, he told himself, he didn't have to drink it all at once. He plunged his arms in up to the shoulders, let the soothing water ease the blistered skin and the rips and tears of thorns and insect bites.

Slocum started to laugh.

He stared at the greenish water as if it were the most beautiful thing he had ever seen. Then, almost in spite of himself, he pitched forward, landing full length in the water hole. He wallowed in it, feeling the water soak his clothes and fill his boots, as if he were conscious of every precious drop.

He turned on his back and lay there with his eyes closed, feeling the water drain the heat from his body. The feverish stiffness of his skin began to soften as his body soaked up the fluid and tried to restore itself, the way a sponge gorges itself on water.

The sound of his laughter seemed to echo from the trees, but it did not seem out of place. He watched a few of the birds on a cottonwood branch arching overhead. Undisturbed by his presence, they chattered to themselves and hopped along the branches from place to place.

Still laughing, he sat up. His legs were straight out before him, and he was waist deep in the water. He scooped some up in cupped hands and drank, more slowly this time, savoring the feel of the water as it slid down his throat. He kicked his feet, watching the arcing water catch a few blades of sun lancing through the branches, turning silver, then vanishing.

When he first heard the click, he wasn't even sure he had. He stopped laughing, and cocked his head to one side. A twig snapped, and he scrambled to his feet. The whooshing of the water slowly subsided into a few small streams, then to intermittent drops.

This time there was no doubt about what he heard.

"You know what they say about countin' your chickens, don't you, Slocum?"

Clay Barrett, a shotgun cradled in folded arms, stood on the bank behind him. Slocum steeled himself for the first shot. He knew he wouldn't hear the second.

10

John Slocum stumbled behind Clay Barrett as he stepped out of the small green oasis into the red glare of the setting sun. Bluish shadows had already begun to creep over the valley floor. The far side of the valley was still brightly lit, but the light was tinged with red. Slocum wondered whether he would have to walk all the way back to the camp. Or if Barrett would kill him rather than put up with the nuisance of dragging him back.

When Barrett had cocked the shotgun, Slocum was certain he had taken his last breath. When the gun went off, he had flinched. Who wouldn't have? And then Barrett had laughed like a spoiled child. It was humiliating, but Slocum thanked his stars. As long as he was alive, there was still a chance.

But he was puzzled. Why didn't Barrett kill him? There was something in the relationship between Bradley and Barrett that seemed out of whack. And somehow Slocum knew that he had a role to play, one that he himself didn't understand but that was significant to the judge and the deputy. It was that, Slocum was certain, and not some unsuspected streak of humanity in Clay Barrett, that had kept him alive. Now all he had to do was to make the most of what, almost certainly, would be his last opportunity.

Slocum was exhausted. Part of him was even glad he had been recaptured. The thought of struggling across miles of high desert, stumbling from water hole to creek to water hole, all the way to Prescott, had been daunting. But he also knew that such gratitude could be deadly. To welcome recapture was to relinquish his freedom. To give it up now, to scum like Clay Barrett and to a blustering fraud like Judge Abel Bradley, made a mockery of that war.

Men had died with less provocation, in response to less humiliation, than that he had experienced at their hands. If he gave up now, they won. And there would be no rematch. Freedom was something you can't lose, but it was also something you could throw away. Half the time you didn't even realize it until it was too late. Slocum knew that he was dangerously close to that point now. And he suspected that Barrett knew it.

If they were bringing him back to the prison camp, it wasn't to kill him, it was to break him. They wanted to strip away the last tattered shreds of his dignity, rub his nose in the dirt, and make him thank them for their attention. Slocum would be damned if he would let that happen. They would have to kill him first. That they were prepared to do so, he had no doubt. How much slack they would give him was something he could only guess at. He hoped he knew the answer before the rope drew him up short and snapped his neck like a dry twig under a heavy tread.

James Allen followed closely on Slocum's heels, prodding him now and then with the handle of his bullwhip. Two hundred yards away, alongside a jumble of boulders, Slocum saw a group of horses. They whinnied and seemed skittish as the three men approached. He cursed himself for his stupidity as he realized what had happened. The men following him had monopolized his attention. Intent on evading them, Slocum had paid no attention at all to the possibility that some of the pursuers had circled ahead. They knew the terrain far better than he did. On horseback, with plenty of water to keep them fresh, it had been a simple matter for them to get to the water hole before him.

Barrett had taken a risk, since he knew Slocum didn't know the lay of the land. But once Slocum had started up the far side of the ridge, it was a foregone conclusion that he would spot the water hole. Having spent several hours under the scorching sun, he would have no choice but to make for it. Barrett had played a cool hand, and it had paid off big.

As they drew closer to the boulders, Slocum realized Barrett had planned carefully. Five horses danced nervously among the rocks. They had taken a pair of fresh mounts for themselves and one for him. Slocum had to admire the foresight. Whatever else Barrett was, he was no fool.

As they reached the boulders, Allen shoved Slocum from behind, sending him sprawling on his face in the dust. He turned, ready to scramble up and take the burly Allen on, but Barrett stepped between them.

"You got a tough row to hoe, Slocum. Don't make it any worse for yourself." Turning to the chubby guard, he said, "Remember what I said, Allen. Don't mess this up."

Allen grumbled, but the words were unintelligible. Barrett looked hard at his underling for a few seconds, as if he were ready to take the fat man on himself; then, with an artificial chuckle, he turned away.

"We better get back. I don't want to be out here in the middle of the night." He reached into a saddlebag on his horse and tugged out a pair of handcuffs. Twisting Slocum's arms roughly, he slipped the cuffs on one wrist, then tugged both arms behind Slocum and snapped the second cuff in place.

Shoving him toward a chestnut with a cheap saddle, Barrett ordered him to mount up. When Slocum was in the saddle, Barrett told Allen to keep an eye on him and stepped back to his own horse. Reaching back into the saddlebag, he tugged a pair of leg irons free of the leather. Stepping back to Slocum, Barrett yanked Slocum's left boot off and clamped one of the leg irons around Slocum's bare ankle. He ratcheted the iron almost tight enough to stop circulation, and, when Slocum complained, he backed off a notch. Walking around the front of the nervous chestnut, he reached under the horse for the dangling chain.

Pulling the other boot off, he shackled the second leg. Slocum was now effectively chained to the horse. Barrett mounted his own horse, and Allen followed suit. Barrett led the way out of the jumbled boulders and began the long trip back. The slope was too steep for the horses, and Barrett followed the valley floor.

Two miles to the west, a narrow gap in the ridge, a dry wash barely wide enough for three men to ride abreast, cut through to the far side. Slocum kept looking up toward the top of the cut. Rocks of all sizes, from pebbles to small boulders, littered the floor of the wash. Now and then, as they edged through in single file, loose rock shifted on the slope or skittered down the steep face of the wash, landing with ominous thuds on the sandy floor.

When they finally made it through to the far side, Slocum found himself staring at Clyde Clemmons at the head of a half-dozen men.

"I got to hand it to you, Clay. You was right," Clemmons said. "I didn't think he had a chance in hell of gittin' this far."

"Don't underestimate Mr. Slocum, Clyde. He ain't at all what he seems to be." He turned to look over his shoulder at Slocum and smiled. "Are you, cowboy?"

"Who is?" Slocum answered.

"Looks to me like Karen almost got what she was lookin' for when she hired you, Slocum. But almost ain't quite good enough."

Slocum was puzzled by the statement, and almost asked

Barrett what he meant, but thought better of it at the last instant. Instead, he just smiled. "We'll see," he said.

"We already seen, Slocum. You come close, but this ain't horseshoes." Barrett kicked his horse into a trot and waved Clemmons and his men to follow him. The sun was on its way down now, and purple shadows filled the desert. It was still light enough to see, and would be for another hour. Slocum assumed, rightly as it turned out, that they were no more than an hour's ride from the camp.

It was just past sundown when the camp came into view. The gate was closed, and Barrett cursed at the sentry when he had to wait for it to be opened. Once inside the fence, Barrett grabbed the reins of Slocum's horse and led the way to a small building in one corner of the compound, just behind the guardhouse. Barrett dismounted and let his own horse wander off while hanigng on to Slocum's.

He called to Clyde Clemmons to give him a hand and handed him the reins. He unlocked one side of the leg irons, walked to the other side of Slocum's horse, and jerked the dangling chain.

Slocum fell heavily from the saddle. His hands were still cuffed behind him. Unable to protect himself, he landed on his shoulder. Barrett kicked him in the ribs, yelling for him to stand up. Slocum rolled onto his belly and raised himself to his knees, twice losing his balance and toppling over before he was able to remain upright.

Barrett reached down and grabbed the cuffs, hauling Slocum to his feet. Pain flashed through Slocum's shoulder, and he wondered whether he might have broken something in his fall from the horse. He refused to let Barrett know he was hurt, and gritted his teeth to keep from groaning.

Barrett shoved him forward, keeping one hand on the chain between the cuffs and jerking Slocum to a halt in front of the small building. Clemmons, trailing behind them, stepped to the door of the small building, unlocked it with a heavy iron key, and pulled the door open. Leaving

Slocum's hands cuffed, Barrett shoved him through the door, nearly cracking his skull on the low door frame. The heavy oak door, strapped with iron bands, slammed shut. When the key ground in the lock again, Barrett hissed through the small grate in the door, "I'll see you tomorrow, Slocum. And you'll wish you never heard of Flat Creek."

"I already do," Slocum whispered. If Barrett heard him, he didn't respond.

Slocum listened to their heavy footsteps as they walked away. When he could no longer hear them, he felt his way around the inside walls of the small building. It wasn't much larger than five by five. The walls were rough wood, and the grate in the door was the only opening to the outside.

Feeling his way carefully with an extended foot, Slocum made it twice around the tiny room before deciding there was no bunk. There seemed to be no furniture of any kind, not even a bedroll. It was already chilly, and he knew he faced a long, hard night.

Exhausted from the arduous afternoon, he knew he'd be able to sleep, but he had no option but to lie on his stomach. Dropping to his knees, he felt the gritty floor through his torn dungarees. Lying down was even harder than standing up, and he turned his head to one side and pitched forward. The impact reminded him of the pain in his shoulder, but he was too damn tired to care.

Slocum slept fitfully for several hours. Each time he woke, he listened to the night. And each time he heard nothing. He might as well have been in the middle of the desert by himself. It was an eerie sensation, knowing that forty or fifty men lay sleeping within a stone's throw. Drifting in and out of sleep, he kept replaying the day's events, wondering what he could have done differently.

And he wondered, too, whether he had been right to trust Carly Duncan. The guy had done what Slocum had asked him to do. But the result was anything but what Slocum had desired. The escape attempt had gone smoothly at first, but he couldn't shake the nagging feeling that it had gone wrong by design, except that the wrong man got blown away. Somewhere in the back of his mind, like a distant voice in a convoluted cavern, over and over he kept hearing the words, *It was supposed to be you. It was supposed to be you.*

He might never know whether it was, indeed, supposed to have been him. But he promised himself, whatever happened tomorrow, it wouldn't be him. The next time, he would make it. And there was going to be a next time. That was one promise to himself he intended to keep.

As the first light of dawn painted the grating a dull gray, Slocum twisted to one side and sat up. He propped himself against the rough wooden wall, staring at the grating, watching it brighten, change color, and slowly catch fire. It wouldn't be long, he knew, before Barrett came for him. He tried to imagine what the big bastard had planned for him. He considered the possibility that Barrett planned to execute him, as an example to the others, but it didn't make sense.

They had killed Martin already. That was all the example anybody would need. It would have been easier to shoot him down at the water hole and let him lie there, slowly rotting in the green water. But that wasn't Barrett's style. And he couldn't shake the feeling that Barrett wanted something from him, or, more likely, that Judge Bradley wanted something from him.

But for the life of him, he couldn't imagine what it was they wanted. One thing was certain: if they did want something, his refusal to give it to them, whatever the hell it was, would keep him alive. His problem was not an easy one. How do you conceal something when you don't know what it is you're trying to hide?

The small square of white light dimmed abruptly, and a second later the key ground in the lock. It must be Barrett. He might not have too long to wait.

The door swung open, the weight of the oak making the

big hinges squeal. For a moment, the sudden glare blinded Slocum. He closed his eyes; then, as they got used to the light, he slowly opened them, expecting to see Clay Barrett in all his swaggering glory. But he was in for a surprise.

The blocky shadow in the doorway was that of James Allen.

"Time to get up, boy." Allen's voice rumbled in his chest, a guttural thunder that reinforced Slocum's impression of a barrel. "You got all the sleep you're gonna get for a while. Git up!"

Allen stepped to one side, nervously, almost expectantly, rapping the door frame with a short wooden rod. Slocum struggled to his feet and slipped into a corner of the small room.

"Come and get me," he said.

"You think I won't, Slocum? That what you think?" Allen laughed. "Well, we'll just see about that, now, won't we?"

He stepped into the solitary cell, again blotting out the light with his bulk. He stepped toward Slocum warily, the wooden rod stiffly extended. Suddenly, with a deft twist, he jammed the rod into Slocum's gut, knocking the breath out of him. Slocum doubled over and coughed, and Allen brought the rod down across the back of his neck, knocking Slocum to his knees.

Reaching down, Allen grabbed the handcuffs by their chain and dragged Slocum out into the morning sun, already ablaze.

"Time to teach you a lesson, sonny boy."

11

Slocum climbed to his feet. As his eyes adjusted again to the brilliant light, he realized the entire company of prisoners stood arrayed in a broad semicircle. At the focus of the arc, a wagon had been turned on its side. The prisoners shuffled their feet, and a nervous hum of whispered conversation buzzed like a distant swarm of bees.

As Allen shoved him roughly forward, Slocum stumbled and nearly lost his balance. He was ready for the second shove, but still felt a stabbing pain between his shoulders where the wooden rod struck just to the left of his spine. The third blow was even more violent, but he sensed it coming and ducked away at the last second.

Allen cursed and grabbed him by the chain. This time Slocum was unable to avoid the blow. Clyde Clemmons and Clay Barrett stood to one side of the overturned wagon. Clemmons held a second pair of handcuffs. He unlocked Slocum's left wrist, and Slocum brought his arms forward for the first time in twelve hours. He rubbed the wrist with stiff fingers to restore circulation, then rubbed his shoulders, trying to ease the ache.

Clemmons waited patiently, until Barrett said, "We ain't got all day, Clyde."

Taking Slocum's right arm, Clyde jacked it up and snapped the open bracelet around the rim of the upper wagon wheel. Slipping the second set of cuffs on Slocum's free hand, he chained it to the wheel some three feet around the rim from Slocum's other arm.

Clemmons stepped away, and Barrett took his place. He leaned in close to Slocum and hissed in his ear. "You are going to regret you ever heard of Arizona, cowboy. But before I'm done with you, you're going to answer a few questions."

Slocum twisted his head to look Barrett in the eye. The big deputy's face was contorted with some secret rage. Slocum cleared his throat, carefully, as if preparing to speak. Then, with a sudden snap of his head, he spat in Barrett's face.

Barrett cursed, and wiped the slime from his cheek with the sleeve of his shirt. He recoiled for an instant, then stepped in, driving his fist into Slocum's gut. The chains of the twin sets of handcuffs jangled, then snapped taut, as they took the full brunt of Slocum's weight. He spun sideways, the pain in his shoulder sockets like hot coals.

For a second, Slocum thought Barrett was going to hit him again, but the deputy turned away. "The rest of you men, pay attention. Mr. Slocum is going to provide you with an object lesson. You got to go along to get along. Mr. Slocum doesn't believe that. Yet. But I guarantee you, in ten minutes he will. And if the rest of you are smart, you will too."

Barrett's thick fingers snaked into his collar, and Slocum winced as the tattered remains of his shirt were ripped away. The cuffs of the shirt dangled from his elbows, the loose threads tickling the skin of his arms. Slocum heard Barrett's feet crunch on the dry sand, then, from a distance, his voice. "All right, Jimmy. Make sure you don't skin him."

Slocum knew what was coming. He heard other steps on the sand, and knew that Allen was taking up his position. Even so, the whistle and sudden crack of the whip startled him. The report next to his ear was like a gunshot. Another close call, this time by his left ear, and Slocum felt a ringing in his head. The noise had temporarily deafened him. He steeled himself for the blow, but it wasn't until he felt the whip bite into his bare back that he realized he could no longer hear the whistle of the lash.

His skin exploded in fiery pain. A second lash, beside the first, spread the fire like gasoline poured on a roaring blaze. Again he felt the whip, and a fourth time. Sweat ran down his rib cage, and his mouth was dry. Slocum tried to swallow, but the cottony thickness in his throat wouldn't permit it.

His back felt sticky, and he knew the whip had broken the skin each time. Two more, in quick succession, and Allen had completed a row across his upper back. Slocum wanted to turn to look over his shoulder, but the whip could take out an eye, and he didn't dare risk it.

His hearing was slowly returning to normal. He could hear whispering, and then the whistle of the leather as Allen started a second tier. Without looking, Slocum knew the man was a master, even an artist. He never hit the same place twice. The skin of Slocum's back was laid open in a dozen places, and the slow ooze of sticky blood was attracting sand flies. They buzzed angrily around his head, and even through the searing pain of the whip, Slocum could feel the insects ripping their hunk of flesh from his bleeding back.

Allen started a third row, and Slocum could hear everything now, as if his senses were heightened. Each curling of the lash sent a hum of anticipation through the other prisoners, and each time it struck, they sighed. It was almost sensual, as if some secret chord were struck in them.

Slocum knew, and accepted it without anger, that the men didn't care if the whipping never stopped.

They were responding like animals, drawing pleasure from his pain. It had nothing to do with him, or with them. As far as the other prisoners were concerned, it could have been anybody, and he was, for the moment, nobody. It was not possible to stand by and watch a person whipped that way. But if you could separate yourself from the humanity of the victim, anybody would respond the same way.

Allen snapped the whip back after the last lash. As if to show Slocum just how good he was, he popped it again over Slocum's head, three times in rapid succession. The noise was explosive, but the pain of his flayed shoulders and back so dominated his consciousness, he barely reacted. Allen walked away. Slocum heard the footsteps recede, but didn't want to turn around. There was a long minute of silence, and then footsteps returned, more sluggish this time, as if they were laboring under a heavy weight.

His curiousity got the better of him. He twisted his head around and canted his body as far to one side as he dared. The first rush of water felt cool on his head and face, but the brunt of it caught him on the raw meat his back had become. It was several seconds before the salt kicked in. The wash of pain as the salt seeped into the open wounds was excruciating. Like a fire deep inside him, it grew, exploding outward until it totally consumed him.

Slocum started to lose consciousness. He felt his body sag toward the ground, the wrench as his arms strained at his shoulder sockets, and then he blacked out.

When he came to, the pain had subsided somewhat. Gradually, he realized he was no longer chained to the wheel. Then, as his senses recovered from the overload, he became aware of his surroundings. He lay in a muddy puddle at the base of the wagon. His back throbbed, but the worst of it was gone. The salt, he knew, would actually help heal his wounds, but he also knew that had been the furthest thing from Barrett's mind.

His body was twisted awkwardly, and as he tried to extricate himself from the jumble of his own limbs, his back brushed against the wagon's lower wheel. The scrape of sand still clinging to the wheel reopened some of the lashes, and the particles of sand gouged into the wounds as if they were eating his flesh.

Only then did he open his eyes again. He lay in shade, protected from the glaring sun by the body of the overturned wagon. The prisoners were gone. A single guard stood by, sitting on the sharp angle of the wagon tongue. When Slocum sat up, the guard ambled away without saying anything to him. Then Barrett reappeared, his swagger somehow less offensive in Slocum's exhaustion. The pain overrode his pride. It took energy to get angry, and Slocum had none to spare.

Poking Slocum with the toe of his boot, Barrett ordered him to get up. His hands were free, and he grabbed on to the edge of the wagon and tried to rise. His arms ached, and every movement of his body made his back feel like it was about to split wide open. The burning sensation seemed to wait for each twist or ripple of a muscle. Biting his lower lip, Slocum swallowed a groan and hauled himself to his knees.

When he climbed to his feet, his head began to swim. The wagon shimmered like a mirage. Even though he had his hands on the dry, splintered wood, the wagon had the ghostly translucence of something more imagined than real. Slocum closed his eyes and blinked, trying to make them focus by sheer force of will. It was like trying to create a world by wishing.

Slocum shook his head, and Barrett grabbed him by the upper arm. "Come on, Slocum, I don't have all day."

The deputy pulled him roughly, and as he lost touch with the wagon, the dizziness returned. Losing patience, Barrett half pushed and half dragged him away from the wagon. Slowly his vision cleared. Things still shimmered, and objects on the periphery were still liquid, but he forced himself to focus on his own feet as he stumbled across the dry, sandy compound.

Just ahead, a short oblong box, its small door open on strap hinges, stood by itself. Constructed of heavy slats, sheeted with hand-beaten tin, and banded with thick strips of iron, like a rectangular barrel, its shadow on the bright sand was a stark smear of black.

Placing one hand on Slocum's head, Barrett shoved him forward and into the box. Slocum had to bend to keep from rapping his head on the top of the door frame. Once inside, he heard the door bang shut. He turned as Barrett slipped a heavy padlock through the latch and clicked it closed.

Barrett stood back a bit and waited. Slocum could see him through the patchwork grille in the door. Inside, on closer examination, he saw heavy oak struts, rough-hewn three-by-threes. As Slocum tried to stand, he bumped his head on the top of the box. But when he tried to sit, he found that the box was too small. In a twisted crouch, Slocum turned back to Barrett, just visible through the small grille. The deputy's face wore a quizzical smile. Half enjoyment and half bewilderment, it was the face of a cruel boy who had just set his first cat on fire and wondered what all the noise was about.

When Slocum said nothing, Barrett stepped close to the box. "You'll find it gets a little warm in there, cowboy. But don't worry about it. It's supposed to. I reckon you'll get thirsty, too. I'll maybe hoist one for you in town later." Barrett licked his lips, as if to swallow an invisible foam. Then, with a mock salute, he turned and walked out of Slocum's field of vision.

The box was already stifling. The small grate permitted no air to circulate. The metal sheathing, unprotected from the sun, turned the interior into an oven. Slocum could feel the sweat begin to run down his body. The raw wounds on his back began to sting as his own salt seeped into the broken skin. Like rivers of fire, the trickles seared their way across his back.

Trying to shift his position, he felt his legs begin to cramp. He was virtually immobilized in the tiny interior. The air grew progressively hotter as the sun continued to beat down on the metal skin of the box. With the door closed, the temperature of the trapped air began to rise.

Slocum tried to assume a crouch, but there wasn't enough room for his legs to fold beneath him, and the effort brought his back into contact with the raw timbers. Leaning forward the few inches he was allowed, he could look out into the compound. It was vacant, and the glare off the sand was white hot. Even through closed eyes, everything glowed a dull red color. Everything reminded him of heat, and the more he thought about it, the hotter he became. He tried making his mind a blank, but there was no avoiding his predicament.

The constant sweating began to leach the fluids from his body. His mouth and throat felt as if they were stuffed with cotton. His breath began to come in short, rough gasps. Every exhalation took a little more water from his body. He found that the closer he came to the metal skin, the higher the temperature. Trying to compress his body into the smallest space and stay at the center of the box took all his concentration. But the harder he tried to stay still, the more he felt himself wavering. In his mind, he became the source of the heat. He could see himself as a flickering light, constantly changing shape, moving from side to side like the flame of a candle.

He could feel the pulsing heat, the throbbing of his blood falling into a rhythm. If he focused on it, the tempo grew faster, and his heart too began to fall into step, beating harder, faster. If he tried to ignore it, then the heat itself pressed in on him, as if he were shrinking away to nothing and the heat were rushing in to fill the void.

He was so thirsty. In desperation, he began to to lick the sweat from his arms. He was enraged to see the precious water trickle down his chest and legs. He sought to trap it with his fingers, letting it accumulate in small pools in the palms of his hands. But when he licked the tiny ponds, the salt only made him thirstier still.

When he thought he could stand it no longer, Slocum pressed his face to the grate and tried to call out. But his throat was too dry. All that issued from his mouth was a meaningless croak. He tried again, still harder, and succeeded only in squawking like a dying parrot. He couldn't even understand his own words.

The muscles of his legs and lower back started to spasm. Movement was all but impossible now. There was no way to relieve the cramping.

The heat seemed like a palpable thing. It pressed in on him like a vise, squeezing him unmercifully. And he knew that it was squeezing the life out of his body. Every drop of sweat became a day, every trickle a month of his future leaking away. In the reflected light coming through the grate, he could count the days of his life ebbing away. He began to wonder just how many days he had left, how many drops.

With a squeak of despair, he reached out with twisted fingers and grabbed the bars. He began to squawk without regard to meaning. The sound was inhuman. Slocum knew it, and he didn't care. That, after all, was the point. Barrett was trying to brutalize him, to strip away every last vestige of his manhood and, beyond that, his very humanity.

He was so far gone, he failed to hear the rattle of metal on metal. And when the dipper, still dripping, its side dewed with condensation, hovered before the grate, he was certain he had begun to hallucinate. Tentatively, trying not to let himself hope, he groped toward the blurry image. His fingers misjudged the distance, and the dipper moved, water sloshing over its sides and wetting his dehydrated skin. Greedily, he brought them to his lips and licked them dry.

Now, frightened that the dipper was the last cruel trick,

he reached for it again. The dipper came close, but it was too large to fit through the bars of the grating. He pressed his face against the bars and the dipper moved slightly, tipping toward him. He caught the first few drops on his tongue. For an instant, he thought of himself as a thirsty dog, lapping at raindrops. Then, as the water gushed from the dipper, he filled his mouth and swallowed. Eagerly, he waited for the dipper to be refilled. When it returned, he drank again.

"That's all for now. You'll make yourself sick." The voice was a whisper, but he was certain he had heard it before.

12

Slocum watched the sky darken. The heat was still unbearable, but the water had saved him. He hadn't seen who it was, but he remained convinced he knew the voice. His arms were numb from the strain of supporting his weight since the morning. All he could think about was getting out of the box.

As the afternoon had worn on, he had turned from the pain to thoughts of revenge. Clay Barrett would pay, and he would pay dearly. But before he could get even, before he could think of so simple a thing as stretching to his full height again, he had to survive. The anger had turned to ice in his chest. It went beyond hate, to something so hard and so cold, it was like a physical presence, down among the ribs and arteries.

When the sun started to go down, sounds of activity drifted to him on a slight breeze. He could hear the gusts of wind sliding past the grate, but the hot air inside the box prevented them from getting inside. He wondered whether it was Barrett's intention to leave him there overnight. And he knew he would never survive a second day. He had been nearly crushed as it was. A second day in the hot box would surely kill him.

As the men returned, he waited for someone to approach the box. He realized it was with a certain pride, pride that he had endured, that he waited. He wanted everyone to see that Barrett had given him his best shot and John Slocum was still standing.

As the brilliant sunset slowly lost its color, the purples and reds turning to an indifferent smudge of bluish gray, footsteps crunched on the sand. A key ground in the lock, but no one was visible through the grate. Bracing himself, he waited for the door to open. It swung outward slowly, and as the air rushed in, he was aware of how foul he smelled.

So far, no one had said a word. Slowly, he released the pressure on his hands and arms. The muscles almost immediately cramped, and he leaned his weight back into them, feeling the spasms slowly subside. This time, more deliberately, he relaxed the pressure, waiting for the first involuntary quiver of his tired body. When one hand was free he did the same with the other, holding his breath and uttering a silent prayer that his body not betray him now.

Leaning forward to duck under the door frame, he stepped out into the cool air. Like a blind man with his sight miraculously restored, he looked up at the sky. The last traces of the sunset, a golden edging to the clouds, glittered like ice, and he sighed. Inhaling deeply, he tried to swallow, but his throat wouldn't respond. His back and legs felt as if he had run a hundred miles.

"I got to hand it to you, Slocum," a soft voice said.

Slocum turned and saw Clyde Clemmons. The guard was shaking his head in disbelief or admiration. Slocum guessed it was a little of both.

"Thirsty," he croaked.

Clemmons nodded. He bent down, and Slocum saw a pail and dipper. He filled the dipper and slowly brought it

to Slocum's lips. Slocum shook his head. He reached for
the dipper.

"Do it myself," he squawked. "Have to."

Clemmons nodded again, as if he understood. Slocum's
hands quivered as he took the dipper. The metal felt as if it
had been frozen. As he raised the dipper to his mouth, the
tremors became more pronounced, and the water began to
slosh over the edge, splattering in all directions. Ignoring
it, Slocum bent toward the dipper and took a slow, tenta-
tive drink. He swished the water around in his mouth. Letting his throat open, he allowed a small trickle to soothe it.
The tissue was so dehydrated, it took a while for the water
to go all the way down.

"Easy, or you'll cramp up," Clemmons said.

Slocum nodded. While he waited for his body to get
used to the presence of water again, he examined the dipper. It was the same one used for his surreptitious drink
that afternoon. He recognized an odd pair of nicks in its
lip, like small triangles, pointing toward the handle.

There was no doubt in his mind it was the same dipper.
But Clemmons hadn't been the one to give him the drink.
It wasn't the same voice. He kept wracking his brain, but
couldn't put his finger on it. He took another sip, this time
larger, and waited for his mouth to lose the cottony feel.
His stomach kept quivering in anticipation, but he fought
the urge to gorge himself.

"Come on, Slocum, I got to put you in solitary."

Slocum shook his head. "Not yet. Thirsty." His voice
was more recognizable now, but still not normal. He
sounded like some animal first learning to speak.

"Look, I got to get you in the lockup. Barrett'd have my
ass if he knew I was taking this long. I'll leave you the
water for a bit, but you got to move along."

Slocum shook his head that he understood. It still hurt
to use his voice. He winced when Clemmons took him by
the arm, and Clemmons apologized. The guard stepped
away, carrying the pail and dipper, and Slocum limped

after him. His calves and thighs ached. His gait was stiff and unnatural, as if the leg muscles had forgotten what they were supposed to do. He struggled to keep up with the guard, but the effort was agonizing.

Clemmons unlocked the solitary cell and stepped inside. Slocum, too tired to do anything else, followed him in. Clemmons set the pail down, the dipper clanking against its side.

"I'll be back later for this," Clemmons said.

Slocum said. "No, wait a minute. Let me drink a little more now, and take it with you." He knelt beside the pail, every inch of the descent stretching stiff muscles. It felt good to be able to move unfettered, even if pain was the inevitable result. Slocum drank deeply this time. He felt his stomach swell with the sudden onrush of water.

"You'll make yerself sick," Clemmons warned. "Look. I'll leave the bucket. I can always tell Clay I forgot it."

"You don't have to do that," Slocum cautioned.

"Hell, I know that," Clemmons snapped. "But there's things a man wants to do every once in a while to make sure he remembers he *is* a man. Sometimes I come close to forgetting."

"How come you work here, anyhow?" Slocum asked between sips.

"'Cause I lost my ranch, is why."

"What happened?"

"Take too long to tell you."

"Who owns it now?"

"I think you can guess the answer to that one." Clemmons turned abruptly, like a man who had just been insulted, and stomped out of the cell. He closed the door with a slam, and snapped the lock shut with a violence that contradicted his gesture of decency in leaving the water. Slocum guessed Clemmons was angry beyond words, and that it had nothing to do with him.

Slocum eased up on the water and got to his feet. He walked to the window and could just make out Clemmons's back in the shadows as he entered the guardhouse. When the guard was gone, Slocum took another long pull on the water, then began to loosen his muscles. He worked slowly, trying to avoid cramps. He worked his arms in tandem, feeling them slowly uncoil. A few deep knee-bends eased the ache in his legs.

His back was another matter. The wounds inflicted by Allen's whip still burned. Tentatively, he explored the skin of his shoulders with his fingertips, then tried, as best he could, to examine his back. Eighteen times he had been struck with the lash, and not one of the cuts overlapped another, as far as he could tell. The sores had clotted, and he no longer bled, but every twist and turn reminded him of each and every wound. The skin would take several days to restore itself. And then, only if he were left alone. Another whipping like that would kill him for sure. If he didn't die of the whipping itself, he was certain to develop gangrene or some other infection.

He lay down on his stomach. There was still no blanket, but after the torture of the hot box, the gritty floor felt as luxurious as a bed in the best hotel in San Francisco or St. Louis. He closed his eyes and cushioned his head on folded arms. It would get cold later on, and he doubted he'd be able to sleep. He needed rest and better get it while he could.

He slept shallowly, waking more than once when he shifted in his sleep and irritated his back wounds. The sudden stabbing pain would kick him awake, and he had to wait until it subsided before he could drift off again.

The fourth time he awoke, he sat up. His back hadn't hurt him, and he wondered what had awakened him. He listened hard, but heard nothing. He changed position and lay back down. But this time he was sure. Someone was at the door.

"That you, Barrett?" he whispered.

No answer. He climbed to his knees facing the door. Whoever it was was still there. Why didn't they acknowledge it? He wished he had his Navy or a knife. Hell, anything, even a hunk of wood, would be comforting. As he shifted toward the wall, his hand brushed against the pail, and he remembered the dipper. It wasn't all that heavy, but if he used it quickly, the surprise might give him an edge. Whoever it was out there wouldn't expect him to have anything at all to defend himself.

Brandishing the dipper, he stepped silently to the door. He saw no one, but it was dark, and he couldn't be sure. He pressed himself against the wall and held his breath. Almost inaudibly, the lock turned. The scrape of metal on metal was muted, and the click of the latch almost as quiet. Had he been sleeping, he wouldn't have heard it at all.

It dawned on him that whoever was opening the door had no business there. Clemmons might have come back for the pail and dipper, but he had no need to be so quiet. Two possibilities occurred to him. Either the person wanted to take him by surprise. Or he didn't want anyone else in the prison camp to know he was there. Neither made too much sense.

But the door squeaked open, and it was too late to wonder about motives. He waited for someone to make an entrance. He heard boots on the sand, but saw nothing. He clenched his fist and tightened his grip on the dipper. There was a soft whisper of cloth, and then a shadow appeared in the doorway. He raised the dipper over his head and waited.

Stepping all the way inside the solitary cell, the shadowy figure pulled the door closed behind it. That answered one question. The visitor was more concerned about others knowing he was there than he was about Slocum.

When the door thudded against its frame, Slocum stepped forward, snaking an arm around the visitor's neck. Summoning all his limited energy resources, he wrestled the man to the floor, letting the dipper fall and clapping a hand over the man's mouth.

Turning the man on his back, he kept one hand over his

mouth and twisted his shirt front in his other fist. For some reason, the surprised visitor wasn't struggling.

Slocum waited, then felt two hands clasp his own. A second later, they shifted, and Slocum heard the snap of buttons being pulled free of their holes. One of the man's hands returned to grab Slocum by the wrist and, insistently but gently, tugged his hand free of the shirtfront. Replacing it on bare skin, the hand guided him, and the surprisingly soft and more surprisingly abrupt slope of that cool skin told him his visitor wasn't a man at all. The breast in his hand nearly made him groan with pleasure. The woman's hand now addressed Slocum's pressure on her mouth.

When he relaxed his grip, the woman said, "I thought you'd be *glad* to see me." It was the voice of the unknown water bearer. And now he knew why it had sounded so familiar.

He slipped his free hand inside the shirt, cupping a second breast, no less cool and no less full. He felt himself stiffen, and stood to pull off his jeans. As he stepped out of them, the woman got to her knees. She grabbed him around the waist and held him.

He felt her lips brush his thigh in a kiss that was both hot and cold. Then, before he could shift his weight, he felt her tongue curl around the head of his penis. It slithered like a live thing along his length, flicking out, tickling, then dancing away.

Slocum inhaled slowly, then held his breath, as if the slightest motion, the least sound, would break the spell she was weaving. Her lips grew slick with saliva, and she nibbled him until he couldn't stand it. Somehow, she seemed to know. The sudden liquid fire that enveloped him took forever to slide home. He'd never felt anything like it in his life. The wetness and the heat, together, made him still harder.

He could still feel her tongue until she started to pull back. Letting his cock slip almost completely away, she plunged her head forward then back, forward and back.

Slowly increasing her tempo, her rhythm steady, each time taking him full length, each time teasing him, almost letting him go. Her hot breath grew agitated, as if she were struggling with something inside herself, faster and faster until he exploded.

She held him tightly around the waist and gave one long, slow last forward thrust of her head. Pulling back even more slowly, she sucked and, with just the tip of his penis still in her mouth, twirled her tongue once more around the head. Then, with a playful, almost childlike exaggeration, she let him go with a loud slurp. She tapped one slender finger on the head of his cock, then sank back to the floor. "I think I owed you that much," she said.

"What you owe me," he said, "is an explanation, Karen."

"Sorry, fresh out. I got some salve for your back, and that's all I've got."

Slocum grabbed her by the arm, and she jerked it away. "You're hurting me," she said.

"Why not. That's what I'm in here for, or did you forget?"

She turned away from him. In the dark, it wasn't possible to see her very clearly, but he thought she might be crying. He reached out a hand and gently rested it on her shoulder. He could feel her shaking until she realized what he had done, then she stiffened.

"Why did you lie to the judge, and to Barrett."

"You saw my face, didn't you? What other reason do I need," she snapped.

"Why did Barrett beat you, then?"

"I don't know. Maybe he likes it. He seems the type."

"So you're not going to tell me, are you? Don't you think I have a right to know?"

"Why don't you leave me alone? Get out of here, why don't you?"

"Because people are being forced off their land, people

are being killed, for God's sake. And Bradley is behind it."

She whirled around. "Their land? Their land? What about *my* land? Don't you think I know what's going on. I'm the first victim, damn it."

"What do you mean?" Slocum was stunned. He watched her closely, not sure whether to believe her. "What land? What are you telling me?"

"I have to go now." He felt her slide away, then heard the rustle of clothing as she got to her feet.

She stepped to the door, and Slocum stayed on the floor, too confused to do anything else. The door creaked open. She stopped, turning to look over her shoulder. He could see her outlined against the night sky.

She tossed a bulky package at him. "Take this. It's all I can give you."

The door closed and she was gone.

Opening the package, he found a box of matches, some tobacco and rolling papers, and a small tin. Examining the latter by matchlight, he found it to contain a thick, bitter-smelling salve. The final part of her gift, wrapped in grease paper, was heavy. He unfolded the wrapping, and knew before it was half exposed that she had somehow managed to get her hands on his Colt Navy revolver. A dozen cartridges clinked against the gun as he finished unwrapping it.

Slocum thought it suspicious that she could obtain the gun, but there were some gift horses better left unexamined.

13

Slocum was up early. The previous night was still vivid in his mind's eye. And he still didn't understand what Karen Alston had told him. What land was she talking about? And how did she lose it?

He hefted the revolver, running his thumb over the grip and slowly turning the cylinder. Almost in a trance, he traced the scene rolled onto the cylinder, feeling each line under his thumb, as if reacquainting himself with the body of a much loved and nearly forgotten woman.

His back felt much better. Whatever was in the salve Karen had given him, it worked. His muscles were still sore, but he felt confident they would loosen up as he worked. The only question was whether he would be allowed to work, or whether he would be forced to spend a second day in the hot box.

As he tucked the familiar weight of the Colt Navy .36 into his boot, he knew the answer to that part of the question. No way in hell would he let anyone stick him back into that oven. He would empty the Colt and make them kill him before that would happen.

He was so surprised at what Karen had told him, he found it impossible to be angry at her. But was she telling the truth, or was it all part of some complex plot?

Amazement kept shouldering his rage aside as he tried to understand why she had done what she had done. And why Bradley had driven her to it. He could understand her passion to recover her land. It was, after all, rightfully hers. He might have done the same in her shoes. Their situations were similar enough that he found himself wishing he had had the chance to do what she was doing.

The only thing that made sense was the possibility that Karen had entered into some devil's bargain with the judge. She must have pledged her cooperation in exchange for her land. On the other hand, he knew that there wasn't a chance in hell Abel Bradley would live up to his end of the bargain. He was using Karen, the way you use any tool. And when she was outmoded, when he had no more use for her, Bradley would throw her on the junk heap. She had to know, or at least suspect, that much. But then, the line between passion for rightful ownership and greed was a fine one. At best, Karen Alston had one leg on either side of the line. She was so used to spreading her legs, he doubted she even knew why anymore.

Tugging the cuffless leg of the prison pants down over the boot, he stood up. There was a bulge on the inside of his right leg, but Slocum doubted anyone would notice it. He walked in a tight circle, stamped his foot a couple of times, and checked again. He had felt the gun shift, its hard metal digging into his ankle, but it was no more noticeable.

Satisfied that he had done all he could hope to do, Slocum sat down to wait. He didn't have to wait long. Barrett hollered to him through the window a minute later.

"Ready for work, cowboy?" Barrett opened the door and stood back. Slocum stayed where he was. He wasn't going to give Barrett the satisfaction. If the deputy wanted him outside, he could damn well come in and tell him so.

"I don't have all day, Slocum." Barrett's voice was brittle, and Slocum knew he was on edge about something. For a moment, he wondered whether Karen had set him up. But he quickly dismissed the possibility. Her story was so incredible, no one would have made it up in an effort to set a trap for him. If they had wanted to use her to trick him, they would have come up with something more believable.

Barrett ducked through the doorway. "Lucky for you we got a deadline, Slocum. Judge says we need every able-bodied man out at the railhead the next few days. We're behind schedule. That means you got to pull your own weight. But I'll tell you right now, we get even, your ass is mine."

"Somehow," Slocum said evenly, "I had you pegged that way right from the start."

Barrett seemed genuinely puzzled. "What the hell are you talking about?"

"Seems like a real man could think of something to do with a woman that didn't involve punching her in the face. Fact, I'm sure he could."

Barrett lashed out with a vicious kick, but Slocum avoided the boot. He laughed, and the beefy lawman swore unintelligibly. He bent down and grabbed Slocum by the arm. "Get up, get the hell up, you bastard. You don't watch your mouth, and I don't give a damn what the judge says. I'll blow a hole in your head that'll make your big mouth look like a pinprick."

Barrett was dangerously close to the edge, and Slocum eased up. He didn't want to give that last push that might tip Barrett into a murderous frenzy. He climbed to his feet and stepped through the door, keeping a wary eye on Barrett, who still grumbled under his breath.

Outside, Slocum joined the jostling crowd from his original barrack. He fell into line to Carly Duncan's left.

He caught Randy Carter's eye for a second, but Carter turned away. The young farmer's face was expressionless. While they waited for Clemmons to conduct the head count, Duncan leaned in his direction.

"You satisfied, Slocum? You wanted to make a break. You see how much it got you. And Martin's dead. What the hell was the point?"

Slocum wondered whether Duncan was right. He hated to admit it, but there was more than a little justice in what the bearded giant said.

"Look," Slocum said, "I didn't make Martin do anything he didn't want to do. And if he hadn't been so damn anxious, we might have made it. It was *his* plan, after all. Don't forget that."

"I won't forget it. Make sure *you* don't."

"All right you men," Clemmons hollered, "straighten up so I can see your ugly faces. And shut up."

Slocum turned toward Clemmons and gave a start. Over Clemmons's shoulder, in a far corner of the yard, Judge Abel Bradley was engaged in a vigorous discussion. Slocum couldn't see who Bradley was talking to, but it looked more than passably like an argument. At one point, Bradley raised his hand as if to slap his opponent. He caught himself, and turned away. Slocum could see the judge's face contorted by anger. And the old man's skin was a bright red, in striking contrast to the brilliant white of his hair.

The judge turned once to hurl a final word or two over his shoulder, then stomped off. Standing there, as if frozen by the judge's words, Karen Alston chewed on her lower lip. It was obvious she had been crying, but Slocum hadn't been able to hear any of the exchange.

He watched the young woman until Clemmons ordered a quickstep to the flatcar. Slocum climbed aboard and took a seat on top of the stack of ties. He stood, craning his neck to see over the fence, but could barely make out the top of Karen's head. She seemed not to have moved at all since the end of the argument. The stack of the small engine belched a cloud of dark gray smoke, and the flatcar lurched. Slocum nearly tumbled from the back of the car, and sat down, where he could get a handhold on the lashings.

At the railhead, Slocum threw himself into the work. He wanted to test his aching body without pushing it too hard. At the same time, he was determined to do nothing to call attention to himself. He regretted that he had been unable to avoid baiting Clay Barrett, but vowed not to repeat that mistake.

As he worked, he felt the Colt Navy scraping away at his ankle. He tried not to think about the gun, for fear he would inadvertently call attention to it. As lunch break drew closer, Slocum started to grow tense. So far, he hadn't seen even the hint of an opening. He had nothing remotely approaching a plan. All he had was the will to escape, and the determination not to get caught a second time. The only thing he knew for certain was that he would do nothing unless he were assured of a horse. A man alone, armed or not, wouldn't stand a chance. He had learned that bitter lesson only too well. And there was a dead man to prove it.

His back still ached from the whipping, but the salve had softened his skin, and Slocum found it possible to work without reopening his wounds. As he and his partner returned to the end of the flatcar for another pair of ties, he spotted a small cloud of dust in the distance. It was moving along the railbed, a few yards to the left. It wasn't possible to see what was raising the dust, but Slocum crossed his fingers. He needed luck as much as he needed a horse.

The two men struggled along the rails and dropped the new set of ties, and Slocum bent to tug them into position, then straightened up with his hands on his hips. He bent backward slightly, to ease the strain on his lower back. He used the opportunity to scrutinize the approaching cloud. It was now possible to see a nucleus of shadow at the heart of the cloud. Two or three men on horseback were coming at a fast gallop.

He saw Barrett jump down from the engine and walk back along the railbed. He waved his partner back to the flatcar, but kept his eyes on Barrett's receding figure. A hundred yards down the track, Barrett stopped to await the approaching riders. As if wondering when lunch would come, Slocum looked up at the sky. He shielded his eyes from the brunt of the sun and grunted. It was still a half hour or so before noon.

Slocum leaned against the end of the railroad car and flexed his shoulders. "I'm blushed," he groaned.

"You and me both," his partner said.

The man was rail thin, his complexion a translucent white. He looked almost consumptive.

"How long you been here?" Slocum asked, trying to prolong the break.

"Too damn long," the man grunted. "Too damn long."

The riders pulled up in front of Barrett, and the dust dispersed. Slocum could now see that he had been almost on the money. There were two men, one of them leading a riderless horse. The lead rider dismounted and began an animated conversation with Barrett. Barrett listened for a couple of minutes, interrupting the man once or twice to ask a question.

When the conversation ended, Barrett mounted the third horse and took the reins from the mounted rider. He pointed in the general direction of the railhead and wheeled his horse almost immediately. Using the reins, Barrett lashed the horse into a full gallop, and the other rider fell in behind him. A moment later both riders were obscured by a new dust cloud.

The newcomer walked toward the engine, leading his horse behind him. When he reached the tail end of the flatcar, he tied the horse to a turnbuckle bolted into the side of the frame used for lashing down the ties. He walked past Slocum and climbed up into the engine.

Slocum climbed up onto the flatcar and wrestled a pair of ties off the stack. They landed with a clatter on the wooden bed of the flatcar, sending a thunderous echo rolling across the open desert. His consumptive partner cursed at nothing.

"Sonofabitch. God, I am so damn tired of this crap."

"Seems to me there ought to be a law against this shit," Slocum agreed.

"Yeah. Well, we ever get a new sheriff, maybe there will be."

"What happened to the old sheriff."

"You ain't the only one wants to know. Somebody bushwhacked Millburn. Backshot the poor sonofabitch. Never did catch the bastard who done it."

"They know?"

"Not for certain. But most folks got a good idea. Supposed to be an election in a couple of months. Trouble is, Bradley counts the votes. And Clay Barrett's running for the job. That makes it pretty clear who's gonna win."

"Anybody running against Barrett?"

"Somebody was."

"Was?"

"You heard me. Two days after Doug Morgan announced he was available, somebody burned his barn to the ground. Three days after that, he left town. Never said a word to nobody."

Slocum nodded. Somehow, the story didn't surprise him. It seemed like the judge and Barrett had a stranglehold on Flat Creek. It wasn't enough, apparently, to own half the land and most of the town. They wanted to own its people, too.

The man walked off, and Slocum turned to the horse. During lunch, he knew, he would have his best shot. He hoped the new rider would stay that long. Glancing at the sun, he guessed he had a half hour. Working on the ties, he got close to the horse, patting him on the flanks every time he came for a new set.

Gradually, the horse got used to him. The animal no longer shied away when he approached. He stroked its neck and rubbed the broad forehead between the eyes, chasing away a few sand flies. With his free hand, he loosed the reins a bit, making sure they would come away easily. Shaking his leg, he felt the two and a half pounds of the Colt rattle in his boot. So far, so good.

When the lunch whistle sounded, he dropped down into the shade a few feet from the horse. One of the other prisoners called to him, but he ignored it. He couldn't take the risk of another man being anywhere near him. And he sure as hell wasn't going to ask for help, leaving a man behind to face Barrett's anger.

He was last in line, and Clemmons grinned at him when the mess crew came around. "Unsociable cuss, ain't you, Slocum?"

"Looking to hang with a better class of people, Clyde."

Clemmons nodded. "You know, Slocum, there ain't nothing wrong with most of these fellers. They just unlucky's all."

"Tell me about it."

"Don't really have to, do I?" He handed Slocum the already familiar cup of warm water. The other members of the mess team walked toward the engine and climbed aboard. Clemmons watched them go, then turned to Slocum. "Watch your back," he whispered, then he too was gone.

Slocum swallowed the water, making a face at its bitter taste. He slipped the tin plate under the flatcar and stood up. Idly, he scratched the horse on its forehead. The animal batted at the hand with a twitch of its nose, trying to encourage him to be more forceful.

The guards were busy with their own lunches, and the

convicts were sprawled in the shade, trying to ease some of the ache in their tired bodies. Slocum hauled himself up onto the flatcar. He sat on the far side of the horse, dangling his feet off the car. Propping one foot on the edge of the car bed, he tugged his pantleg up and slipped the Colt out of his boot. He tucked the gun in his belt and covered it with his shirt.

Slocum lay down, then rolled to the end of the car, dropping to the ground as quietly as he could. So far, no one seemed to have noticed. He stepped toward the horse, which turned toward him. It started to shuffle nervously until Slocum reached out to pat its neck. Using the body of the horse to screen himself from the others, he reached for the reins and uncoiled the last loop from the turnbuckle.

The horse, sensing that it was no longer hitched to the railroad car, backed away a step. Slocum slipped one foot into the stirrup, and pulled the reins over the horse's head. Swinging into the saddle, he kicked the horse into a gallop, leaning forward to press himself flat along the animal's neck. He heard a shout, but ignored it. Kicking the animal again, he got it moving flat out. The horse seemed to sense his urgency, and Slocum could feel the animal straining to run still faster.

This time, Slocum knew, there would be no reprieve. Barrett hadn't gotten around to asking his questions, but whatever he thought Slocum knew would be less important than revenge. They would bring him back dead, if they bothered to bring him back at all.

Glancing over his shoulder, he saw the guards spill out of the engine. When the first shot whined over his head, he kicked the horse again and yanked the Colt from his belt. He fired once, then again, sending the men diving to the ground. He waited for the first man to scramble to his feet, then fired a third time. The man fell, but Slocum couldn't tell whether he had been hit or simply dropped to the ground in self-defense.

The others began firing wildly. Already beyond range of the shotguns, he had to hope nobody got lucky. For good measure, he emptied the Colt, then turned his attention to the terrain ahead of him. Looking up at the unforgiving sun, he knew that this time there was no turning back.

He'd have to kill Clay Barrett. And it would be a pleasure.

14

Slocum waited until nightfall. When he was certain they hadn't picked up his trail, he mounted the stolen horse and headed for Flat Creek. It was nearly ten o'clock when the town suddenly appeared in front of him. He couldn't help but remember his first visit. His relief at reaching civilization had been misplaced, to say the least.

He sat on the outskirts, waiting for the last light to go out. The flickering orange of the kerosene lamps was mesmerizing. The hotel, naturally, stayed lit longer than anyplace else. From his vantage point, he could see its upper two floors. He assumed the saloon was still open, as well.

The first step would be to get his own horse back. He had been trying to decide what the second step could be. One after another, he considered and rejected a number of options. Some of them were pointless, and some just plain loco. Few of them had much chance of success. And none of them sat right.

He couldn't shake the feeling that there was something he had to do, but he'd be damned if he knew what it was.

That was where instinct took over. He played cards with his gut as well as his head. In fact, he thought, he lived his whole life that way. There might not be any other way to do it, at least for him.

When the last light went out at the back of the hotel, Slocum nudged his stolen horse forward. The terrain surrounding Flat Creek was as flat as a tabletop, and there was no place to hide. A couple of trees and a few saguaro afforded the only cover. Dismounting, he tethered the horse to the trunk of a cottonwood. His first stop was the livery stable.

Slipping up from the rear, he found the double doors barred, but otherwise unlocked. He looked for another door, not wanting to wake the dead with the infernal squeak of the rusty strap hinges on the big stable doors. A smaller door, held shut with a simple gravity latch, was more appealing. He opened the latch and slipped inside. The horses started to shuffle nervously in their stalls. They sensed him, but were undecided whether he posed a threat to them.

He groped around for a lantern and found one hanging on a rusty nail just about head high on the wall inside the door. On a cross strut, his groping fingers found some dry seed and a few mouse droppings, but nothing more. Reaching around the other side of the lantern, he found what he was looking for—a box of wooden matches.

He took the lantern down and squatted on the floor, fumbling with the chimney, then realized he better not light it until he absolutely had to. If he were really lucky, he might not even need it. But a steady light could attract attention he didn't need.

He carried the lantern with him, but settled for striking a match to get his bearings, then snapping it and crushing it underfoot. Holding the lantern and matchbox in one hand, he used his other, still clutching a few matches, to guide him along the stalls.

Working his way along the right side of the stable, he

kept hoping the liveryman hadn't sold his horse. Word about his immediate future was probably common knowledge. But the stableman had seemed like a decent sort. He would have held the horse for a few days, at least. He better had. One after another, Slocum lit his matches, checked the stall on either side, then moved two stalls down and did it again.

So far, he came up empty. At the far end, closest to the street, he reversed himself and crossed to the other side. The first match revealed a tack rack, and among the assorted reins and saddles he spotted his own. The gear, at least, was still there. Now if he could only find something to put it on.

Midway through the second row of stalls, he struck pay dirt. The big roan stared at him past the flicker of the match. In the horse's huge eyes, Slocum thought he saw recognition. He eased the stallion out of its stall and quickly saddled him. Before putting the bit in, he found, by matchlight, a feedbag and offered the horse some oats. The roan stuck his nose in, snorted, and shook it off. At least he had been fed. Slipping the bit in, Slocum looped the reins in place and buckled them.

Slocum draped his bedroll and saddlebags in place. On a sudden thought, he opened the saddlebags and tugged out a small leather drawstring pouch. He hefted it, then loosed the string and dumped a handful of coins into his palm. He picked out a dollar, and slipped it into the matchbox. The livery man would find it in the morning. When he realized Slocum's horse was gone, he'd probably make the connection. If not, not.

Tugging the horse toward the rear doors, he looped the reins a hitch just inside. As he stepped toward the small door to slip outside, he was startled by a sudden burst of light. He heard the rasp and sputter of the match as he turned. The livery man stood there, a Colt .44 clutched in one fist, a sputtering candle in the other.

"I seen you leave the buck, or I'd a shot you already."

His voice was steady, and amused more than irritated.

"You sleep here?"

"Sometimes. I'm lucky at that. Folks around here have a tough time holding on to things. Least I got the stable. For now."

"Bradley?"

Instead of answering, the old man stuck the Colt into his belt. "Might as well give me that lantern, son." He reached out for the kerosene lamp.

Slocum took a match from the box, but the old man shook him off. "I'll use the candle." He lifted the chimney and lit the wick. A small column of oily black smoke rose up until the flame caught. He adjusted the wick and dropped the chimney back in place.

In the soft light, he looked younger. Slocum realized it was the spirit in his face. The dull lamplight obscured the wrinkles in the old man's leathery skin. He hung the lantern on a nail, then turned back to Slocum.

"You plannin' on movin' on, I guess?"

"Soon," Slocum said.

"You ain't thinkin' of doin' somethin' stupid, I hope. You look the type."

"I don't like the way I been treated. Seems like it might be a good idea to make that point before I leave."

"I wouldn't."

Slocum nodded. "Most folks wouldn't, I suppose. But I had my share of being pushed around. Man's got to draw a line someplace. Here's as good as any."

"Unless I miss my guess, you drawn more than a few already."

Slocum said nothing.

The old man didn't need an answer.

"You mind if I move along?" Slocum asked. "I don't want to hang around here any longer than I have to."

"I expect they'll be looking for you."

"Unh-hunh."

"You got any help?"

"Don't need any."

"You must be something special. Never met a man couldn't use help. You think maybe Clay Barrett ain't as mean as he looks?"

"Doesn't matter."

"You change your mind, you let me know. I might be old, but you can't live forever anyhow."

"I might do that."

Slocum climbed onto his horse and yanked his carbine from the boot. The Winchester magazine carried a dozen .44-40 cartridges, and he took as good care of it as he did the Colt Navy. He returned the carbine to the boot. "You mind gettin' the door, old-timer?"

"Name's Reilly."

"Fair enough. You mind, Mr. Reilly?"

The old man slipped through the small door, and Slocum heard the bar thump on the ground. Reilly opened one door just wide enough for Slocum to ride through.

He walked the horse along behind the building on the main street. Dismounting behind the hotel, he tethered the horse. There was a back door to the hotel at the head of a set of rickety wooden steps. He climbed carefully, placing each foot down slowly. He avoided the thump of boots on the wooden stairs, but it wasn't possible to mute the squeak.

On the small landing, he tried the door. It was paned with pebbled glass. A dim light shone through from inside. Slocum tried the knob. It squawked, but he ignored it, tugging the door open with a jerk of his arm. It opened easily, and he slipped inside.

Closing the door almost all the way, he peered out through the last crack. There was no sign that anyone had seen or heard him. He listened for a moment, then pulled the door all the way closed. His steps were muffled by thick carpet as he moved down the hallway. When he got to Karen Alston's room, he stopped to listen. Taking off his hat, he pressed his ear to the door panel. When he heard nothing, he tried the knob. It rattled, but wouldn't turn.

Slocum ran his fingers along the top of the door frame and found a key. He tried it on the lock, and it slid in easily. The knob turned, and he opened the door as quietly as he could, pressing on it with an open palm.

He closed the door softly.

As he crossed the carpet, he heard the rustle of bed-clothes. "Is that you?" Karen whispered. "Clay?"

Slocum said nothing. He stepped quickly to the bed and sat down on its edge. In the darkness, he felt her begin to caress him.

"Clay, honey? Say something, why don't you?" Her hands encountered the gunbelt. She sat up abruptly. "I told you, I don't like you wearing a gun here, Clay."

"You never told *me* that," Slocum whispered.

Karen gasped. He reached for her, clamping one hand over her mouth and holding the back of her head with the other.

Leaning toward her, he hissed, "Are you waiting for him? Is Barrett coming here tonight?"

She shook her head in the negative. Squeezing her head tightly, he asked again, "Is Barrett coming here tonight?"

This time she mumbled through his hand, "Unh-unh!" She shook her head even more vehemently.

"If I let go, will you promise not to scream?"

This time she shook her head positively. "Are you sure?" Slocum demanded. Again, a yes.

He began to release the pressure. He felt her inhale sharply, but she made no attempt to cry out. Relaxing the pressure still further, he felt her lips form a kiss against his palm. "Forget it," he snapped. "That's finished."

He let go completely.

"Why?" she asked.

"Why what?"

"Why is *that* finished?"

"I have more important things to do."

"You mean I'm a distraction?"

"Of a kind, yes."

"Then why are you here?"

"I want to ask you some questions."

"Can I put the light on?"

"It isn't necessary."

"I'd feel better..."

"What the hell. Go ahead, but keep it low."

He felt her weight shift on the bed, and the mattress sank beneath her. Her movement rustled the sheets, and a soft fragrance surrounded him.

He listened to her fumbling with the lantern. "Do you want me to get it?" he asked.

"Would you?" Her voice was husky, and he felt himself stirring, in spite of his resolve. Grateful for something to occupy both his mind and his hands, he reached for the lantern and took the chimney from her.

She thrust a match into his other hand. He popped it with his nail, and quickly dipped the flame toward the wick. Slocum turned the flame down a bit and replaced the chimney. Only then did he permit himself to look at her.

With a coy smile, she dropped the sheet she held bunched at her neck. "Distracted?" she asked.

"No," he lied. "You seen two, you seen 'em all."

"Bastard..." She got to her knees on the bed, and her weight pulled him toward her. She wrapped her arms around his neck. Slocum smiled. He reached for her chin and cupped it in his hand.

"That's more like it," she said, flicking her tongue at one corner of her mouth.

She seemed surprised when he pushed her backward on the bed, more surprised still when he straddled her, kneeling on the mattress. His knees bracketed her rib cage, accentuating the thrust of her breasts.

"Aren't you going to take your pants off?"

"I always talk with them on."

"Talk? But I thought..." She slapped at him, but he

caught her wrist gently, then refused to let it go.

"I know what you thought. But I already told you. That's finished. You owe me a few answers. That's all I want from you."

"You sonofabitch, Slocum." She was so angry, she was barely intelligible. If I were a man, I'd . . ."

He reached down with his free hand, brushing her nipples with the back of one finger. "You wouldn't have these." He grinned at her. "And if you were a man, I wouldn't have to be here in the first place." He shrugged. "But you aren't a man, and I *am* here. So . . ."

She sighed. "You're sure?"

"Yes."

"We could . . . you know? I mean, we really could. I'd answer your questions . . . afterward."

"No."

"Damn you, Slocum."

"Yes," he said.

"Maybe another time?"

"Maybe."

She sighed again. "All right, what do you want to know?"

"If I think you're lying to me, I guarantee you'll regret it."

"Understood." She let her hand rest on his thigh. "Ask away."

"What did you mean about the land?"

"Like I told you, it's mine. Half of it, anyway. When my daddy died, his half was supposed to come to me. It was in his will."

"What happened?"

"I was underaged. The judge was the executor of the estate and a trustee of my inheritance. The rest, as they say, is history." Slocum listened in silence. It was all too familiar a story. And this time, he knew, Karen was telling the truth. Perhaps not all of it, but she wasn't lying.

"Clay Barrett said he wanted to ask me some questions. What did he mean?"

She hesitated. Her fingers began to slide along his thigh, but he grabbed her wrist and held it. "What did he mean?" Slocum asked again.

She struggled to free her hand. "You're hurting me, you bastard. Let go!"

"I warned you," Slocum said. His voice was just above a whisper, but there was something in it that frightened her. She stopped struggling.

"He thinks you were hired to kill Judge Bradley."

"That's ridiculous!"

"It's what he thinks, though."

"How do you know that?"

"Because I know someone told him so."

She looked up at him, and in the dim light of the lamp, Slocum could see the traces of tears glistening on both cheeks. Her eyes had become sparkling pools.

"How do you know?"

"Because..." She sniffed, then wiped her nose on the back of her free hand. "Because...I'm the one who told him."

15

Slocum hobbled his horse below the crest of a low rise. He looped the reins of the stolen horse over his saddle horn and snugged the loop tight. He dropped to the ground and squirmed up to the crest. The binoculars were already hot to his touch. He raised them to his eyes and watched the engine chuff the last three hundred yards to the railhead. It looked like business as usual.

Training the glasses on the engine, he counted the guards as they dropped down to the ground. The four men stood idly, their weapons gripped a little more tightly than usual. They kept darting their glances from place to place. At this distance, they looked more like nervous ducks on a pond than prison guards.

Sweeping the glasses slowly to the rear, he spotted two more guards on the flatcar. The guard contingent was lighter than usual. He would have expected increased vigilance after his escape. It made no sense, unless the others were out looking for him. The guards were easy to spot, since the prisoners wore uniforms.

On a hunch, he checked the faces of the prisoners he could see. He didn't know all the inmates, but it didn't appear that Barrett had tried to surprise him by disguising a few guards in prison uniforms. The work detail was as large as usual. So far, the breaks had been going his way.

With the exception of Clay Barrett and James Allen, Slocum had no grudge against the guards. They were just men doing a job, one most of them didn't particularly like. But when your land is taken away, and you have no other way to put food on the table, you have some hard choices to make. Slocum tried to put himself in their place. Being honest with himself, he wasn't sure what he would do if he had to make the same decision. It wasn't easy either way.

Slocum was grateful that he hadn't had to kill anyone ... yet. With Barrett and Allen, he just might make an exception. The thought of gunning them down in cold blood wasn't attractive. But he wondered whether it could happen any other way. Neither of the bastards was the type to fight fairly.

He would see.

And he would do what he had to do.

The work gangs formed up, and they began the back-breaking day's work. Down on the flat, it would be difficult to take the guards by surprise. But the chances of doing it any other way were pretty slim. And Slocum knew the longer he waited, the more likely the odds against him would increase.

He hadn't told Karen Alston what he planned to do. But it wouldn't be hard for her to figure out. And if she didn't, or couldn't, Barrett surely would. He still didn't know what moved her to do what she had done. That she was desperate, he was certain. That she was doing something she found distasteful was less so. After all, she obviously had some relationship with Clay Barrett. If there was a connection, Slocum didn't know what it was. He didn't know for certain that Karen would tell Barrett about his visit, but he had to assume she would.

He had long ago given up trying to understand people. And women were even more difficult to understand than men. He'd tried more than once to puzzle his way through a situation with a headstrong or devious woman at its center. Each time, she had sat there like a spider, attuned to every bounce of the web. Sometimes she denied there was a web, and sometimes she claimed she was caught in it just like he was. Always, she had sworn he wasn't a fly. But not once had he been able to see all the way through to the end.

That Karen Alston was at the center of this web could not be disputed. But whether it was of her own spinning was another question entirely.

Lying there on the ridge, he watched the activity at the railhead. Slowly the line extended, and slowly it was made permanent. He could hear the ringing of the sledges, a strange, hollow sound drifting across the desert. Scanning the work gangs with the glasses, he looked for Randolph Carter. Before he did anything, he wanted to know where the young farmer was. He finally spotted Carter on his second pass, near the head of the work gang, lugging ties with Carly Duncan.

For reasons he still didn't understand, Carter had stuck his neck out to help him. The kid no longer seemed willing to talk to him, but that was understandable. People sometimes do what they have to do, without considering the consequences. Carter had helped him, and Slocum was determined to balance the ledger before he left Flat Creek. Once Carter was free, that would be the end of the matter.

As he watched, he wondered what moved Bradley to his mania for the railroad. The limited water, Flat Creek itself, was all there was. It meant that the town couldn't grow much larger than it already was. The farms were hardscrabble, and every irrigation ditch reduced Flat Creek to a smaller trickle.

Slocum understood a love for the land. When the land was your own, that love was a passion like no other. If things had been a little different, if justice had been as blind as she was supposed to be, Slocum would be two thousand miles from this godforsaken place, hacking at his own soil.

But justice wasn't blind. She peeked out from behind that twisted rag to see where the power was and only then did she make up her mind. To people like Carter, and Slocum himself, she turned a blind eye and a deaf ear. For bastards like Bradley, she climbed into bed and spread her legs.

To spend your life chopping at soil so dry it could blow away in a stiff breeze seemed to him madness. But that was Carter's choice. Carter had the right to live or die on his own land in his own way. And no one, not Clay Barrett and not Abel Bradley, had a right to take it away from him.

Slocum realized there would never be a good time to do what he had to do. The only way was to jump in with both feet and kick anything that moved. He slid back down below the crest and unhobbled his horse. He patted the big roan on the flank, then climbed into the saddle. He left the stolen horse tethered to his saddle horn. He loosened the Colt Navy in his holster and pulled his hat forward on his head. It was about all the cover he was going to get.

Kicking the roan into a trot, he crested the rise, then angled down the far side. The rocky soil, littered with cactus and slippery under the roan's hooves, kicked up little puffs of sandy dust. Once or twice, one of the horses slipped, and the sand got deeper as he neared the flat. It was going to be a tricky maneuver, but riding straight to the idling engine was his best shot, perhaps his only one.

It was nearly a mile to the railhead, and if he got lucky, they wouldn't notice him until he was in close. The roan wanted to run full out, but Slocum kept a tight rein, holding the dust to a minimum. The trailing horse was less feisty, and Slocum could feel it tugging at the reins as they lashed at his leg. In the brilliant light, he would be almost

on top of the engine before anyone could recognize him.
What happened next was up to fate.

Without the binoculars, the men straggled along the
work front were little more than dark spots in the blinding
glare. Now and then a bright flash of polished metal spar-
kled in the sun as a rail was maneuvered on the end of the
crane. The sound of the hammers grew louder. He kept his
eye on the front end of the work crew, where Carter had
been dropping ties.

He closed slowly, hoping no one spotted him until he
was close enough to seize the initiative. Once he got in
tight enough for a dead shot, all he needed was one target.
Given a choice between living or dying, most men would
choose to live. Dying to keep a man you didn't know in a
jail where you knew he didn't belong was just plain dumb.
Slocum was counting on that fact to even the odds a little.

At two hundred yards, a scurry of activity told Slocum
they had spotted him. He felt the Colt still on his hip and
hoped he didn't have to use it. At a hundred and fifty
yards, a man ran toward him, flapping his arms. In the
glare, it was impossible to recognize the approaching man.
Slocum tilted his hat forward still more and slowed to a
walk.

At seventy-five yards, he recognized Clyde Clemmons.
The guard still didn't seem to recognize Slocum. At thirty
yards, he dismounted, keeping his face averted. As Clemmons approached, the guard yelled, "Howdy. You a long
way from noplace, partner."

Slocum smiled. Clemmons was a decent man, and that,
too, might work in his favor. He stepped toward the rear of
the roan and pretended to examine its left leg. Dropping to
one knee, he slipped the Colt out of its holster and held it
loosely against his calf.

"Havin' some trouble?" Clemmons asked. The guard
was no more than fifteen yards away now, and still closing.

"Some," Slocum mumbled.

"He pull up lame, or just pick up a stone?" Clemmons

seemed relaxed, just a man trying to be helpful. He knelt beside Slocum and said, "Here, let me take a look at that."

"No need, Mr. Clemmons," Slocum said. He felt the guard tense up, and as he turned, the Colt in his hand, he prayed Clemmons wouldn't do anything stupid.

"Slocum!"

"Sorry, Clemmons, but I got no choice."

"You must be loco, comin' back here. Barrett'll kill you."

"Barrett ain't here."

"What do you want?" Clemmons asked. He seemed nervous, but not frightened. That was a plus. Fear made men unpredictable. If Clemmons kept a grip on his nerves, he wouldn't do anything crazy.

"All I want is Randy Carter. He don't belong here, and you know it."

Clemmons said nothing.

"Now," Slocum said. "Ease your gun out and hand it to me. Then stand up."

Clemmons nodded. He reached for the revolver on his hip, gripped it in two fingers, like a kid holding a dead mouse by the tail, and pulled it free of his holster. "Here," he said, handing the gun to Slocum.

"I'm sorry about this, Clyde," Slocum said.

"I'll bet."

"I mean it. You were fair to me, and I appreciate that."

"You gonna shoot me, ain't you?"

"No. But it's best that your friends believe I will."

Clemmons grunted.

They moved toward the train, Clemmons walking just ahead of Slocum, shielding him with his body. So far there was no indication that the other guards suspected what was happening. The closer Slocum could get, the easier it would be.

The work gangs were still busy, and the relentless ring of hammers on spikes seemed to increase its frequency, keeping pace with Slocum's racing pulse. Clyde Clemmons was a big man, three or four inches taller than Slocum, and his broad shoulders all but concealed the man behind him.

When the engine was ten yards ahead, Clemmons stopped. Without turning, he asked over his shoulder, "What do you want me to do?"

"Go to the front of the engine. And keep your mouth shut. I don't want to hurt anyone."

"What do you want, then?"

"I want Randolph Carter, I already told you."

"How come?"

"He's only here because he tried to help me. I don't know what Bradley and Barrett are up to. But if they got a beef with me, it's with me, not Randy Carter."

"You spring him, and they'll just bring him back. You can't stay here forever. And Carter don't want a nursemaid anyhow."

"Maybe you're right, but I have to try. I owe him."

"Whatever you say."

"All right, Clyde, now hold on. I'm gonna get right behind you. I hate to do this, but I don't see any other way." Slocum stepped in behind the bigger man and wrapped his left forearm around Clemmons's neck. He jabbed the muzzle of the Colt Navy into the base of the big guard's spine. Clemmons winced, more from surprise than pain.

"All right," Slocum whispered, "walk around to the front of the engine."

Clemmons did as he was told. As they turned the corner, two of the guards were leaning against the front end of the flatcar. Two more were intent on watching the work gang at the head of the flatcar. Counting Clemmons, that made five. Where the hell was the sixth man?

"Who's missing, Clemmons?" Slocum hissed.

"Bill Culver."

"Where is he?"

"Right here."

Slocum turned to see Culver, a revolver in his hand, lean down from the engineer's window.

"I suggest you give it up right now, Mr. Slocum. It'll go a whole lot easier on you."

Slocum laughed. "It hasn't been easy so far, Culver. I don't expect things'll change anytime soon. Now, unless you want me to blow Clemmons a new asshole, you better toss that gun on down here."

"You know, I can tear your head off with one shot, Slocum."

"Maybe, but if Clyde lives, he's never gonna walk again. You want that on your conscience, you go right ahead and shoot."

"He ain't bullshitting, Billy," Clemmons said. Slocum wondered whether the big man really believed he'd be shot, or if he was just doing his damnedest to make sure he wasn't.

Slocum stared at Culver. The guard's hand wavered just the least little bit, but that was all Slocum needed to see. If he hung on long enough, he knew Culver would pack it in.

"Slocum, I call the other guards here, and you're a dead man."

"So's Clyde. And I'll tell you what. I bet I can put one right through your head after I shoot Clyde. How about it, Culver, you a betting man?"

The guard's upper lip glistened with sweat. Clemmons shifted nervously from foot to foot, but made no attempt to free himself from Slocum's grasp. "Come on, Billy. Throw it down. He only wants Carter. Nobody has to get hurt."

"Especially you, huh, Clyde?" Culver laughed. He shook his head, then said, "Oh, shit! Here." He tossed the gun to the ground.

"All right," Slocum said, relaxing a bit. "Now, climb out through the window, so I can see you."

Culver wriggled through the small window, almost losing his footing on the narrow metal bar that encircled the engine. He dropped heavily to the ground, then turned to face Slocum. "What now?"

"Get Carter, and bring him back here. And be careful. Clyde ain't home free yet."

"You won't get far. You know that, don't you?" Culver asked.

"Maybe I won't. But, hell, I got to give it a shot. Wouldn't you?"

Culver seemed puzzled by the question for a few seconds. He shook his head, then said, "Hell, I guess so."

Slocum watched Culver walk toward the work gang. Carter was walking back toward them, and Culver raised a hand to call him over. The two men talked for a few seconds, then Culver turned and headed back toward Slocum. Carter trailed right behind him.

When Carter realized what was happening, he looked baffled. He started to speak, but Slocum motioned to him to keep quiet. He pointed to Culver's gun. Carter stared at it for a long time. Finally, Slocum hissed, "Pick it up, damn it!"

Carter looked as if he were going to refuse, and Slocum barked again, "Pick it *up!*"

This time, Carter did as he was told. "Now what the hell are we going to do?" he asked.

16

As Slocum and Carter rode off, they watched over their shoulders. The guards, horseless and disarmed, jumped down from the flatcar and milled around. No one would pursue them on foot, but they knew it was only a matter of time before a posse was assembled. Some of the prisoners rushed into the desert, willing to take any chance at all rather than endure another day in the prison camp.

As they hit the rise, Slocum slowed his horse to negotiate the tricky ascent. When he reached the crest, he turned and waited for Carter. The farmer was less than expert as a horseman, and his mount picked its way carefully, heedless of Carter's random sawing on the reins.

Slocum grabbed the binoculars and examined the chaos across the valley floor. In the distance, he spotted a cloud of dust, about five miles from the railhead, probably additional guards, maybe even Clay Barrett himself. Slocum smiled thinly, his lips compressed to a pale, narrow gash in his immobile face.

When Carter reached the top of the hill, he pulled up. Slocum nudged his horse closer.

"You know they'll be looking for us, don't you?"

Carter nodded. "Yeah, I know that."

"We can just ride out of here."

Carter shook his head. "No way. I can't leave my sister. Besides, the farm is all I have in the world."

"Bradley will get it eventually, you know." It was stated matter-of-factly, but Carter disagreed with a vehemence Slocum had not seen in him before.

"The hell he will."

"You think you can stop him?"

"Not by myself, I can't, but, yeah, he can be stopped."

"You'll need help."

"What's in it for you?"

"Satisfaction." Slocum knew, as soon as he said it, that that was what it was all about. To cut and run, whether Carter came with him or not, made Bradley the winner by default. "Anybody in town you can count on?"

Carter took a long time in answering. "Maybe." His face was grim, but the set of his jaw spoke of determination. "Maybe we should go back and release the others."

"You think I didn't think about that? But there's no way. Maybe later, when we get some help."

"Sooner or later, I'm coming back here, with or without you."

"Okay. But right now we got a more immediate problem. Where to?"

"My place."

The ride to Carter's farm was grueling, nearly thirty miles across barren, waterless wasteland fit only for the snakes and lizards that lived there. Slocum kept a watch over his shoulder, stopping on high ground every few miles to survey their wake. He had seen no indication that they were being pursued. If anyone was chasing them, he was careful not to betray himself.

Slocum was impatient. He wondered whether it made

any sense for him to stick around. It wasn't, after all, his fight. The people of Flat Creek had sat back and watched Bradley walk all over their neighbors, using the law when possible, and goons when necessary. He already had more land than he could ever use, and that wasn't enough. Slocum knew that mentality. And he knew that no amount of land was ever enough for such men.

On the other hand, he had sprung Randy Carter. In that sense, they were even. And he couldn't hang around babysitting Carter for forever. If Carter couldn't handle it, he didn't belong in Flat Creek anyway. If he could, he didn't need Slocum's help. But the more he dwelled on it, the more he knew he was trying to convince himself of something that wasn't true, something he could never believe. Carter was now a fugitive from justice. It was true that the justice was perverted, but if anything, that meant Carter was in more jeopardy, not less.

Bradley and Barrett were unforgiving men. And they couldn't afford to let Carter walk away. It was a chink in their armor they had to patch. If Carter could get away with it, so could anyone else. The trickle would become a steady flow and then a flood. Bradley and his dreams of empire would be swept into the desert by the torrent.

By the time they reached Carter's farm, they were exhausted. The sun was brutal, and Carter was unused to extended periods in the saddle. He was half standing in the stirrups to ease the pain. Slocum pulled up and called to Carter.

"We better take it slow from here on. Barrett's no fool. He might be waiting for us."

Carter nodded. "What should we do?"

Slocum swept the glasses across the horizon. The house itself, a simple wooden affair, looked deserted. A barn, its new wood still green, also seemed empty. There were no horses in sight, but Barrett would have been smart enough to leave his mount out of sight.

Flat Creek lay just below them, no more than thirty feet

wide, snaking through a land so dry it was a wonder the whole thing didn't just sink into the sand and disappear. Slocum followed the course of the stream with his glasses until it disappeared into the rolling foothills to the north. Beyond, still glittering with snow, several tall mountains, probably fifty miles away, explained the source of the water.

"How in the hell can anyone make a living farming here?" Slocum asked.

"Flat Creek is sweet water," Carter answered. "There's enough. I irrigate. I can raise enough to feed us, and to run a few head of livestock. It ain't much, but it's enough."

"Too bad Bradley doesn't see it that way."

"He's a dreamer. In a way, it's too bad. I think, when he started, he meant well. Things got out of control, that's all."

"You're a more understanding man than I am, I guess," Slocum grunted.

"Anyhow, when you come from someplace where you have nothing at all, even this little bit seems like a blessing. There's a future here, and that's something I'm still getting used to."

"I guess." Slocum was unconvinced. "Look, I'm going to head upstream and come up behind the house. Take these and watch me." He handed Carter the binoculars. "If it's all clear, I'll wave my hat."

Carter nodded. "And if it isn't?"

"I haven't got that far yet." Slocum grinned.

Carter returned the grin, smiling for the first time since the trial.

Flat Creek was bordered on both banks by brush and tangled greenery. In most places, it was tall enough to conceal a man from someone on the opposite side, if he was careful. Slocum nudged his roan down to the bank and headed upstream. Under the clomp of the roan's hooves, he heard an occasional gurgle as the creek worked its way through the jumbled boulders that marked its course.

A quarter mile upstream, Slocum found a break in the green wall and eased the roan down the bank and into the water. The creek was no more than two feet deep, and in many places it wasn't half that. He kicked the roan up the far bank and dismounted. He took off his hat, dropped to his knees, and buried his face in the water. He drank deeply. Even though the water was warm, he realized Carter was right. The water was sweet. There was no trace of the bitter alkali that so often made high desert streams undrinkable, and worthless for farming.

When he had slaked his thirst, Slocum slipped through the foliage and tugged the horse after him. Once through the tangled growth, he climbed back into the saddle. The open land between the farm and Flat Creek was dotted with patches of green, but they were small and sparse, mostly cholla and gnarled bushes full of thorns to protect their small, thick, waxy leaves.

From behind, the house still seemed deserted. Slocum tethered his horse in a small stand of saplings, at the end of an irrigation ditch. On foot, he approached the house, keeping an eye on the barn as well. When he reached the house, he looked for Carter, but the sun was too bright for him to see through the glare. At the back door, he tried the string latch. The door swung open, and he stepped inside. It wasn't much cooler inside, but at least the sun was off his back.

He found himself in a combination kitchen and living room. A couple of dishes on the table still bore traces of food. The food was still moist. The dishes had been used within a couple of hours. Pushing through a beaded curtain to the left, he found himself confronted by two doors. Carefully, he opened the nearest. It was a small bedroom, sparsely furnished with a makeshift cot and a small table. Clothes, obviously Carter's, hung on wooden hooks mounted on one wall. A small window let a block of glaring white light into the room, where it lay like a thing on the floor.

He backed out and tried the other door. This was also a bedroom. It sported a bed with a hand-carved walnut headboard, obviously hauled from back east. Calico curtains framed the small window. An ornate wardrobe, its carvings nicked and chipped, supported a mirrored door. The mirror's silver had cracked and crazed, but it still lent a touch of femininity to the room.

Slocum pulled back out of the room. He saw himself in the mirror before the door closed, and realized he was smiling. He felt guilty, as if he had somehow violated its owner. He remembered Sissy Carter from her visit to the jail, and he felt his smile broaden.

But she was gone.

Slocum stepped out onto the plank porch, his spurs jingling like a music box. He felt vaguely silly, tiptoeing around an empty house, but then he realized there was a purpose to his caution. He looked for Carter again, and still saw nothing. Carter, he knew, would be able to see him through the binoculars. He reached for the brim of his Stetson, but stopped when he heard a horse neigh in the barn.

He jumped off the porch and sprinted toward the barn. The door was open a crack, and he debated whether he should go inside. Framed against the bright sunlight in the doorway, he'd be a perfect target. Instinctively, he drew the Colt halfway out of its holster, then let it settle back.

Instead of using the main door of the barn, he walked around to the side of the building, looking for some other way in. A wide window, its frame partway open, caught his eye. He tried to pull it further open, but it wouldn't budge. He moved on around the corner and found what he was looking for. A small door, its latch held shut with a padlock slipped through the latch ring, was set in one corner of the back wall of the barn.

Slocum pulled the lock out and opened the latch. He tossed the lock to the ground and flattened himself alongside the door. With a jerk of his arm, he flung the door open. Waiting a minute, he listened. No sound came from inside the barn. Backing away, Slocum got a running start and dove through the open door. He landed on his shoulder and rolled, coming to rest against a stall in a pile of ripe-smelling hay.

His eyes adjusted slowly to the gloom. He drew the Colt and squeezed his eyes shut, trying to force them to adjust. Getting to his knees, he heard a muffled moan. Squinting through the darkness, he tried to pinpoint the source of the sound. On a hunch, he dropped to his belly and squirmed forward a few feet. He no longer heard the noise.

Something moved in the shadows. He heard a shout. A body hurtled toward him, and he swung the Colt but held his fire. A thicker, darker shadow stirred across the barn, and the sudden flash of a muzzle caught him by surprise. The bullet slammed into the stall just to the left. In the brief flare, he saw the familiar, squat figure of Jimmy Allen. Slocum squeezed off a shot, and the heavy Colt bucked in his hand. He fired a second time and was rewarded by a cry of pain.

Allen fired again, but the shot went wide, and Slocum aimed into the halo left by the muzzle flash. This time, Allen went down. His gun clattered on the hard-packed dirt floor of the barn. Slocum waited, listening. The body on the floor to his right stirred, but it was the only source of sound. Slocum crawled to the door and flung it open. Sunlight poured in, and in the sudden glare, he saw Allen's crumpled bulk, a dark red stain spreading beneath it.

Across the barn, moaning, lay Sissy Carter. Slocum rushed to her side and knelt down. Her shirt had been torn nearly off. Bright red scratches covered her chest, as if she had been clawed by an animal. He pulled the pieces of her shirt together, draping them as best he could over the ample breasts, and brushed the tangled hair from her face.

"Are you all right?"

She moaned, and he bent closer. A dark bruise shadowed one cheek. The eye above it was swollen. She tried to sit up, and Slocum slipped one hand under her shoulders, supporting her. As she sat up, the shirt fell open, and Slocum tried to cover her again. She got unsteadily to her knees; then, as if just recovering consciousness, she jerked her head and opened her mouth as if to scream.

"It's all right, Sissy. He's dead. It's all right." Slocum was whispering, trying to calm her down.

Instead of screaming, she collapsed into his arms, burying her face in his shoulder. Slocum patted her back, his rough hands uncertain just what they ought to be doing.

Sissy sobbed in fits and starts, as if the terror in her was too large, had to be disassembled and brought out piece by piece. She tried to stand, but Slocum held her down. She struggled against him, and he let her go. As she rose, her breasts brushed against his lips, and he turned away, unnerved by the feeling.

When she was on her feet, he stood. She stared at him as if trying to place him. "I know you from someplace," she said. "I've seen you before. What are you doing here?"

Then, as if aware for the first time that she confronted a strange man while half naked, she fumbled with the remains of her shirt, folding her arms across her chest to hold the fragments of cloth in place.

Instead of answering her, Slocum took off his hat and walked to the door. He stood framed in the opening, waving the hat. When he turned back, he found himself staring down the barrel of Allen's revolver. The ugly gun was gripped tightly in an unwavering fist. Despite the beautiful woman who held it, it was still a deadly weapon.

"Up," she said, gesturing with the pistol that he should raise his hands.

Slocum did as he was told.

17

Sissy Carter sat down at the rickety table with a sigh.

"Didn't go well, did it?" her brother asked.

She shook her head. "No, it didn't. I asked everybody I thought we could trust, and you know what they all told me?"

"I can guess," Carter said.

"They told me there was no way to beat Bradley. They said that if we tried, he'd kill us, and that anybody who helped us would be as good as dead. Owen Reilly offered to ride to Prescott for the federal marshal, but I don't know if he will or not."

"Some awful big hearts here in Flat Creek," Slocum said.

"They're good people, Slocum," Randy snapped. "You got to understand how tough it is for them."

"I understand how tough it is for them... now. What I can't understand is how they let it get that tough in the first place."

"What do you know about it?" Sissy shouted. "You

141

come waltzing in here like some hobo, and now you want to pass judgment on everybody. If it wasn't for you, Randy wouldn't even be in this mess. He didn't have to help you, but he did."

Slocum nodded. "That's true. He did. But that was yesterday. What I'm talking about is tomorrow. You don't stop Bradley now, you might as well gift-wrap the deed to this farm and send it on over to him. You want, you can deliver it personal. But you better be on your hands and knees. Otherwise, Judge Bradley might think you're getting uppity. Where I come from, politicians don't think too much of uppity folk."

"Talk about yesterday," Sissy said, fixing Slocum with a withering sneer. "You forget, you lost the war. 'Uppity' isn't a crime anymore."

"You tell that to Judge Bradley," Slocum said quietly.

"Look, this is getting us nowhere fast," Randy said. He turned to his sister. "Look, Slocum got me out. He didn't ask me to help. I did that on my own. And it was Clay Barrett and Judge Bradley who sent me away, not Slocum. Now all he's trying to do is return the favor."

"We don't need favors from the likes of him."

"For Christ's sake, Sissy, the man saved your life!"

"I didn't ask him to, did I?"

"Damn it!" Randy banged his fist on the table and stood up. "We still got a problem here. Barrett is gonna be lookin' for me. We got to figure what to do about that." He walked to the window and pulled the curtains aside to look out at the sunset.

"I'll tell you what to do about that," Sissy shouted. "You can go get Clay Barrett right now. Tell him where Slocum is and tell him to come get him. Barrett doesn't want you. He wants Slocum. You know that as well as I do."

Randy spun away from the window. When he spoke, his voice was barely audible. "You say that again and, I swear to God, I'll haul you out to the woodshed and—"

"Look, maybe it's best if I push on, anyway," Slocum cut in. "Maybe Sissy is right. Maybe Barrett will leave you alone once I'm gone."

"You don't believe that any more than I do. And Sissy doesn't believe it either." He sat down at the table again and took her hands in his own. "Do you?" he asked.

The young woman bit her lip. Unable to speak, she looked first at her brother, then at Slocum. Finally, she shook her head. "No, I don't believe it either," she whispered. "I want to, but I can't. Oh God, Randy, what are we going to do?"

"I don't know," her brother said.

"There is one thing we can do, Randy," Slocum said.

"What's that?"

"Who usually helps you? Somebody who stands to gain by it himself, right?"

"So, the people in town already said no."

"They're not the only ones who stand to benefit."

"Who else?"

"The prisoners."

"You must be crazy. We'll have the Army here, we try that."

"I don't think so. Look, Bradley threw me in jail on a trumped-up charge. He jailed you just for wanting to tell the truth. I got to believe that at least some of the other men in that work camp don't belong there any more than we did. If I'm right, Bradley doesn't want the territorial administration or the federal government to know what he's doing. He can't afford it. Probably end up doing time himself, anybody found out what was going on."

"So what?"

"So if we can get some of the prisoners on our side, it'll be us against Bradley. Plain and simple."

"Barrett will kill you both," Sissy said. She brought her hands to her mouth, as if to wipe away the meaning of her words.

"No, Slocum's right," Randy said. "But how the hell do we manage to pull it off?"

"We go in the middle of the night. They won't be expecting anything like that, so we should have the advantage. If we can manage to get a handful of men armed, that should be enough."

Carter looked doubtful. "It's awful risky."

"You got a better idea, I'd love to hear it," Slocum said. "In the meantime, we have to round up a few weapons. If we're going to make a run at the compound, we'll have to arm several of the prisoners."

Carter shook his head. "I got a carbine and two revolvers, that's about it."

"Not good enough," Slocum said. "Anyplace we can get a few more guns?"

"I have two pistols," Sissy volunteered. Slocum could tell by the look on Randy's face that it was news to him.

"Where'd you get them?" Randy asked.

"One was Dad's. He gave it to me before he died."

"What about the other one?" Randy persisted. "Where'd you get it?"

"It doesn't matter. I got it, that's all."

"I want to know where—"

"Maybe you two can sort that out later," Slocum suggested.

"Butt out, Slocum. It's family business." Randy slammed the table to emphasize his point.

"I said forget it," Sissy snapped.

"Look," Slocum insisted, "regardless of where it came from, we need that gun. But we still don't have enough. Two rifles and four pistols is not going to do the trick."

"So how many more do we need?" It was Sissy who asked. Slocum was surprised. She seemed to be the more aggressive of the two. It wasn't unheard of, but it still seemed odd.

"At least four more. There's always at least a dozen men in the guardhouse. If we want to make sure nobody gets hurt, we need firepower. If the guards think they can outgun us, they'll try. We have to make sure they understand they're on the short end."

"I can get them," Sissy said.

"Where?" Randy was incensed. "Where the hell can you get four guns? What's going on here?"

"Never mind. I'll get them, that's all you need to know."

Before Randy could say anything else, Slocum cut in. "Do it! How long will it take?"

"An hour. Maybe a little more." She stood up. "I think maybe we should keep watch. And sleep in the barn. When I get back, we'll ride to the prison."

"That's a good idea," Slocum agreed. "Our best chance should be just before daybreak. Randy and I will take turns watching during the night."

Before her brother could object, Sissy was out the door. They heard her horse for a minute or two, and then silence.

"That's a brave woman," Slocum said.

"That's a fool, you ask me. I don't know what's going on here, but I sure as hell don't like it."

"Beggars can't be choosers, Randy. I know you're upset. But try to keep a rope on your feelings until we're finished. You pay too much attention to them, somebody'll get hurt. We don't want that to happen. We got to play this by the book."

"I guess."

"You think Reilly will actually get the marshal from Prescott?"

"I don't know. He's a good man, but that's expecting maybe too much. Reilly's old. He don't have much of a stake in this business anyhow."

"Why don't you turn in? We can bring some blankets out to the barn. I'll take the first shift. I'll wake you in a couple of hours."

Carter stood up. Without saying a word, he disappeared through the beaded curtain. Slocum heard his boots on the rough wooden floor, and he was back in five minutes, several blankets held to his chest.

They extinguished the lamp and lugged the bedding to the barn. Carter made a bedroll for himself and carried it to the loft, where he scraped some straw into a low mound and spread the bedding.

Slocum sat inside the barn door on a pile of straw. He spread a blanket out and busied himself cleaning and loading the weapons they already had on hand. The smell of gun oil hung in the air around him. The soft glow of the metal in the dim light was almost comforting. He felt like a miser counting his coins. And like a miser, he knew he was a little short of what he wanted.

Randy was snoring by the time Slocum finished cleaning the weapons. He sat back and listened to the younger man's unsteady rumble echo from the rafters.

Sissy returned a half hour later, lugging a heavy saddle-bag.

"You get what you were after?" Slocum asked.

Sissy nodded. She set the bag down in the straw. "I guess," she said.

She dropped to the straw beside him, sitting easily, with the grace of an Indian. "I want to apologize," she whispered.

"No need."

"Thank you."

"Quiet night," Slocum said.

"It's so damn quiet it makes me crazy sometimes. It's like me and Randy are the only people in the world."

Slocum studied her profile in the dim moonlight. There was no mistaking her kinship with Randy Carter. Her features were like a softer version of Randy's own, the nose more delicate, the chin rounder. She was exquisite.

"I guess I owe you more than an apology. You saved my life," she said.

"Forget about it," Slocum said.

She reached out and took his hat off, then clapped it on

her own head. "How do I look?" She turned to the side, then stared at him, as if studying his face for something other than words.

"You're a beautiful woman, Sissy."

She took the hat off and leaned toward him. He thought she was going to kiss him. He yelped when she nipped his nose with her small teeth. "Got you," she laughed. Then, leaning close again, watching him flinch, she pressed her lips against his. Her tongue flamed into his mouth, and he responded with his own.

"Make love to me," she whispered. Before he could answer, she backed away and pulled her shirt over her head. The magnificent breasts glowed like burnished copper in the moonlight. She grinned impishly and cupped her breasts in her hands, accentuating their lushness.

He leaned forward and caught a nipple in his mouth, nipping it with his teeth. "Got you back," he mumbled, the words almost muffled as he sucked the dark areola fully into his mouth. He worked his tongue in feverish circles, feeling the nipple harden. She took his head in her hands and guided him to the other breast, then lay back, pressing him to her as she collapsed into the straw.

While he sucked her breasts, he felt her fingers working at his buttons, and he hunched his shoulders to let her remove his shirt. She fumbled with the gunbelt and belt, then unbuttoned his pants. He reached for her, and found her hands already loosening her own belt. She arched her hips as he slid his hand down into her dungarees. Her bush was thick and silky, its tight curls already damp.

He let her breast slide away, feeling its saliva-slick nipple slip past his cheek. Tugging her dungarees down, he got them to her knees and she lifted her legs and kicked them free. Taking his head in both hands, she guided him to her stomach, where his tongue flicked like a serpent's, sliding into her navel, then on down through the sweetly fragrant moss.

She spread her legs, and he buried his face between

them. Licking and probing, he explored every slippery crevice with his eager tongue. She moaned, and her legs spread wider still. He lapped greedily at the musky juice, its salty taste and pungent aroma exciting him still more.

She fumbled with his cock, but he was intent on tasting her to the full. Her hips rose in the air and she began to buck faster and faster, keeping pace with his tongue. She moaned, and the flash flood drenched his lips and chin. She tugged him back, and he spun to kneel between her still arching thighs. With urgent fingers, she took his shaft in both hands, guiding its potent length toward home.

He teased her with its tip, slipping in and out, just ahead of her clutching lips. She gasped and let out a small cry of frustration. Suddenly, almost angrily, she closed her legs around his waist. Her hands on his hips pressed him down and in. Plunging full length into her at last, he wondered why he had waited so long.

Her hips rose to meet him, then fell away. Their urgent rhythms quickly meshed, and he thrust deeply and slowly inward, then out again. Driving each thrust a little faster, bone hammering on bone, flesh slapping against flesh, he listened to her breathing and the hungry sucking of their juices as he rode home. He was gasping for air, the rough pant of his breath raspy in his throat.

Sissy moaned and urged him on, her clenched fists hammering at his loins. She writhed beneath him, her strong legs clasped still more tightly around him. He could feel her muscles clutching at his penis, enfolding it, reluctant to let go then opening to greet each new penetration and once again refusing to give him up easily. Her own breathing was ragged, and she chewed now at the back of one closed fist, trying to muffle the sound of her own cry of pleasure.

"Oh God, Slocum, oh God, oh God . . ." She broke off with a choking sob, and he felt himself explode inside her. She went limp beneath him, but refused to let him withdraw.

"Stay there, stay there, please. I'll feel so empty."

He let his weight down gently, supporting himself on his elbows. He stared into her face, seeing himself reflected in the twin pools still glistening tearily in the moonlight.

"Promise me something," he whispered.

"What?"

"Promise me we'll do that again."

She wrapped her arms around his shoulders, half rolling him from side to side. "Of course we will," she laughed. She tightened her muscles playfully, tugging at his slowly shrinking erection, teasing it back to attention.

"Promise me something too, Slocum?" she whispered, kissing his closed eyes.

"Anything you want."

"This is something special, though. So I want it on a platter."

"What is it?"

"On a golden platter."

"Okay, okay," Slocum said, feeling himself stirring deep inside her, beginning to grind his hips in slow circles. "On a golden platter. What is it you want?"

Sissy responded with an arching of her own hips. As Slocum began his first long, slow thrust, she whispered in his ear, "Clay Barrett's head."

18

A single lantern dangled outside the guardhouse. Slocum led the way on foot. Their hobbled horses snorted restlessly, uneasy at being left alone in the nighttime desert. Intent on the shadows cast by the lantern, Slocum was only dimly aware of Randy and Sissy behind him. At a hundred and fifty yards, he waved them to the ground and dropped to his stomach. Training the glasses on the murky darkness, he waited for a movement, some slight realignment of the jumbled pattern of orange light and deep black shadow.

He listened intently but heard nothing. Neither he nor Randy knew enough about the nighttime habits of the guards. Slocum was not happy with a cold run, but on the long ride, they had been unable to come up with anything better.

He wondered, too, about Sissy. Ordinarily, a woman would be a liability on a mission like this. But Sissy was no ordinary woman. Instead of bone, her supple flesh seemed to have been molded around a frame of steel and ice. Slocum had to trust her because he had no choice. But in the back of his mind was the unsettling reality that if she failed to pull her own weight, she would drag him and Randy down with her.

The plan was simple; he hoped it wasn't simpleminded. They would surprise the sentries, disarm and lock up the guards, and set the prisoners free. There were horses enough for most of the men in the corral. Some of them could double up, and the rest could use the wagons. Beyond that, Slocum hadn't bothered to think. He hoped it wasn't because they wouldn't get any farther.

Slocum crawled closer to the compound, waving Randy and Sissy after him. At a hundred yards, he spotted the first sign of life. The brief flare of a match, followed by the intermittent glow of a cigarette. It had been too quick for him to get a look at the guard's face.

He eased closer, still not certain how they would get inside the fence. They carried wire cutters, but they would be a last resort. If they had to go over the fence across the compound from the guardhouse, they would then have to cross the open area between the barracks and the gate. The moon was half full, but in the clear air, its light was too bright for safety.

He saw the arc of the cigarette, shooting sparks as it spun up and over the fence. Using the glasses again, he examined the gate. It was locked, and its shadow on the dull beige sand showed a thick chain looped across the slight gap where both halves met.

He crawled back and whispered to Sissy, "How do you feel like being the bait?"

"Do I have any choice?"

"None that I can see."

"All right." There was no trace of hesitation in her voice. "What do you want me to do?"

"Get your clothes dirty, muss your hair. You want to look like you've been wandering around out here for a few hours. Get the guard's attention. When he opens the gate, keep him occupied. Whatever you do, make sure he leaves the gate open."

When she was ready, Sissy pecked him on the cheek, kissed her brother on the forehead, and walked slowly toward the fence. She dragged one leg as if it had been injured, and if he didn't know better, Slocum would have thought she had been wandering for hours, exhausted and near delirious.

He couldn't hear anything, but watched her closely through the glasses. He saw the guard walk toward the gate, one hand on his sidearm. Then, when the guard realized what he was seeing, he seemed to relax. The chain was removed, and the gate pushed open just wide enough for Sissy to step through.

Slocum saw the guard reach for the gate, ready to pull it shut, when Sissy collapsed, falling forward into the sentry's arms. The unwary man slowly lowered her to the ground, then knelt beside her. He leaned forward, as if to hear some whispered words, then seemed to fall over on his side.

Slocum got to his feet. He heard Randy behind him, and the two men rushed toward the gate. As they reached the gate, Sissy stood up. Swiftly, Slocum slipped through. Sissy smiled at him, her eyes glittering in the moonlight.

He looked at the guard prostrate on the ground, lying on his side. He seemed to be curled around himself, and Slocum realized why. The rusty handle of a kitchen knife prevented the guard from falling all the way over. In the moonlight, the blood pooled in the sand looked black as coal. His shotgun leaned against the fence. Randy picked it up.

Slocum looked at Sissy. She shrugged, but said nothing. Slocum stepped to the corner of the guardhouse. A second sentry sat on the ground, leaning back against the wall, smoking a cigarette. Slocum stepped softly. Without looking up, the guard said, "That you, Cal?" not imagining it could be anyone else.

Slocum stuck the muzzle of the Colt Navy in the guard's right ear. The guard froze. Slocum dropped to one knee and leaned toward him. "Cal's dead," he whispered. "You want to join him?"

The guard tried to shake his head, but the gun made him reconsider. Slocum disarmed him, handing his revolver to Sissy. Randy took the Remington double-barrel from against the wall. Slocum rapped the sentry with the butt of the Colt. The sentry slumped to the ground.

"Sissy, let the men out. Randy and I will disarm the other guards. Give them the guns we brought and send them over here."

He and Randy handed her the pistols and the weapons taken from the guards, except for the two shotguns, which they kept for themselves.

When Sissy got halfway across the compound, Randy took the lantern from its hook. Slocum opened the guard-house door and stepped inside. A dozen men lay sleeping in their cots. Randy set the lantern on a makeshift table. Rapping the butt of the shotgun on the floor, Slocum woke the men. They sat up, disoriented, rubbing the sleep from their eyes.

"Gentlemen," Slocum announced. "You know what this Remington can do. Unless you want to see a demonstration firsthand, you'll all cooperate."

Carter collected their weapons, piling them on the floor near the door. He also gathered several pairs of handcuffs. When the weapons had been assembled, Carter began cuffing the men in pairs, snapping one bracelet, slipping the chain through the iron bars of a bunk, and cuffing a second man to the first.

Before he finished, Sissy arrived, leading several prisoners. She distributed the captured weapons to the milling convicts. When the last pair of men had been cuffed, Slocum ordered everyone outside, except for the captured guards.

"Gentlemen, I would suggest that you make the best of

a bad situation. We don't want anyone to get hurt. The prisoners are free to go. They won't hurt you. Someone will be here in the morning to turn you loose." He backed toward the door, kicked it open, and stepped outside.

The convicts buzzed angrily, and Slocum realized that several men were agitating for some more permanent revenge to be exacted. "Hold on, now," Slocum hollered. "Listen to me. We didn't turn you loose to harm those men. You're free to go. You have some weapons, and there are horses and wagons available. If you know what's good for you, you'll put as much distance between you and this place as you can manage by daylight."

"What about Barrett?" Carly Duncan demanded. "That bastard ought to pay."

"Look, I'm not telling you what to do, I'm just telling you what I think is smart. You do what you want. All I ask is that you leave those men in the guardhouse alone. They can't hurt you, and, for the most part, they were just doing a job."

"Tell it to the judge, Slocum," Duncan shouted.

"I intend to do just that," Slocum said softly.

Several of the men laughed. "Slocum's right," somebody else shouted. "Let's get the hell out of here." He turned toward the gate and led the way toward the corral.

As Slocum walked through the gate, he turned and looked back at the barracks.

"What's wrong?" Sissy asked.

"I was just thinking," Slocum said. "Now comes the hard part."

First light came suddenly. Slocum sat by himself, peering out through the crack between the barn doors. He could see the house clearly, but its approaches were out of his line of sight. The limited visibility made him uncomfortable. He climbed the ladder to the loft, trying not to wake Randy or Sissy.

He stepped past Randy, and moved past Sissy on tiptoes. She was sleeping on her side, and the sight of her profile reminded him of what had happened a few hours before. Instinctively, he wiped his face. The scent of her still clung to his skin. For a second, he thought about waking her. It would have been foolish, and he knew it. Pushing the urge aside, he moved past her. She stirred and mumbled something in her sleep.

Slocum stood stock-still. Sissy rolled over in her sleep. When she had settled down, he stepped past her to the loft door. It was closed, but he knew that leaving it open would be less suspicious than having the huge doors on the ground floor wide open.

He undid the simple latch and, holding onto the door with one hand to keep weight off the hinges, let it swing open. He did the same with the second door, then stepped back. With the binoculars, he could see nearly a hundred and eighty degrees. Almost dead center, the road from Flat Creek stretched out beyond the house. Like the track of some giant snake, it wound in tight semicircles across the dry floor of the valley.

To the left, Slocum could see Flat Creek itself, its placid water reflecting the rising sun. It looked like a band of flames as it meandered through the dry countryside. He raised the binoculars and twiddled the focus knob until he had a clear image. Starting with the roof of the house, he swept the field of vision. He didn't know what he was looking for, but the sense that something was about to happen raised the hair on the back of his neck.

From left to right, then back, he worked the glasses in overlapping arcs. The valley was still partially in shadow, the purple color of the night collected in hollows and depressions. The high desert gave the false impression of being tabletop flat. Under the midday sun, the brilliant glare scoured all irregularities away. It was only under the morning and evening sun, when the light came in at an acute angle, that the slightly rolling terrain revealed itself for what it was.

He heard a rustle in the hay behind him and dropped the glasses to his chest. He turned to see Sissy watching him. He smiled at her, and she mouthed the words, "Good morning." He nodded, and she stood up. As she tiptoed through the hay in bare feet, he realized just how long her legs were. Viewed from his haunches she seemed to tower over him. Her shirt was half unbuttoned, its tails dangling down over her dungarees. The coal-black hair was tangled, and woven with stray bits of hay. She looked even more beautiful than he remembered.

She squatted down beside him, not bothering to fuss with her hair or clothes. Almost unconscious of her beauty, she seemed completely devoid of vanity. Her uncomplicated view of herself and her place in the world simply enhanced her appearance.

"See anything?" she whispered.

"Nothing."

"You're sure they'll come here, aren't you?" It sounded more like a statement of fact than a question. He took a long time before he answered.

"Yeah, I'm sure. They can't afford not to."

She nodded as if she understood.

"You're not sorry about last night, are you?" he asked.

"It was my idea," she said. "Remember?"

"Yeah, it kind of was, I guess."

She balanced herself on one knee and draped an arm across his shoulders. "Look, Slocum . . . John. I'm a big girl. It wasn't exactly my first time, you know."

"I know that. But . . ."

"Don't worry about Randy. He doesn't have anything to say about it. And if you'll feel better, he doesn't even have to know." She started to rub his shoulders as she spoke, almost instinctively. The motion was so natural, he knew it was something she had done before, and often.

"You keep a lot of secrets from him, don't you?"

"He's my brother, not my chaperon. I don't pry into his affairs. I don't know who he goes to bed with, or when, or, for that matter, whether he does at all. That's his business. And I have a life that has nothing to do with anybody but me. I'm entitled to that, and if he can't accept it, it's his problem."

"I understand. But I wasn't talking about your sexual habits."

"What then?" Even whispered, the question had an edge to it.

"The guns. Randy isn't the only one who wants to know where you got them."

She stopped rubbing his back and drew her hand away quickly, as if it had been burned. "And I'll tell you what I told him. I got them. That's all you have to know."

"Is it? Is it really?" Slocum turned to look at her, and she turned away angrily.

"Yes, it is."

A bright flash caught Slocum's eye, and he raised the glasses. He saw nothing at first, but was convinced he had seen something. Sweeping the glasses in a narrow band, he scrutinized the area where he thought he had seen the flash.

"You better wake Randy," he said.

"What is it?" Sissy's voice had lost its edge. The anger was replaced by concern.

"I'm not sure. Maybe nothing, but . . ." He shrugged.

Sissy walked over to her brother and knelt beside him. Shaking him by the shoulder, she said, "Randy, get up. Randy. *Randy.*"

Slocum heard the young farmer stirring. Randy groaned and sat up. "What is it? What's going on? Slocum?"

"I don't know. Wait, there it is again. Somebody's coming."

Slocum twiddled the knob on the glasses, trying to sharpen the image. In the reddish light, everything was blurred, and a rainbow framed the edges of the lenses, further obscuring things.

A few moments later, he caught his first glimpse. A rider, looking back over his shoulder, flashed up over a low mound and disappeared down the other side. Seconds later, several more riders came and went the same way. The glimpse was too brief, and the image too fuzzy, for Slocum to identify any of the horsemen.

"Five or six men, maybe seven. I can't be sure. They're about two miles away. You got the horses hidden?"

"Yeah," Sissy said. "They're down by the creek, about a quarter mile downstream."

"Okay, you keep out of sight. Randy, grab one of the carbines and set yourself up. Make sure you can cover this side of the house and most of the open space between here and the porch. I'll cover the rest."

"I think I'll go down. I can see better from there, and I'll feel a whole lot better. I feel like a trapped rat up here."

"And what happens if they search the barn?" Slocum asked.

Randy shrugged. "Then somebody gets shot."

Sissy said, "Randy, for Christ's sake, will you listen to Slocum. You're so damn pigheaded sometimes. You always know what's best."

"I just don't like it up here. There's no place to run if we have to."

"If they don't see us, we won't have to run," Slocum reminded him.

"All right, all right. Jesus." Randy kept grumbling to himself until he settled down behind a pile of raw lumber. Bracing the carbine against one end, he would be able to cover most of the yard.

Slocum took up a position in the opposite corner of the open door. He could see what Randy couldn't. Between them, they had the entire area between the house and barn under their sights. "Look," Slocum said, "whatever happens, stay here. We don't shoot unless they do."

"I heard you," Randy snapped.

The riders were close enough to be heard. Slocum looked over his shoulder to find Sissy. She was in a far corner of the loft, crouching behind a pile of old tack.

Slocum felt his palms dampen. The barrel of his Winchester grew slippery. He wiped his hands on his shirt and chewed at his lower lip. He hated waiting more than anything else. He found himself remembering the endless waiting of the war. It seemed like every engagement required two or three weeks of interminable bivouac, a forced march, then more waiting. Every man in his unit had begun to come unglued. They actually looked forward to the combat, glad for however brief a time to have something real to do, some use for their hands and outlet for their nervous energy.

The first rider appeared beyond the house now, his horse kicking up sprays of sand as he galloped toward the farmhouse. Hard on his heels, the others, in a tight knot, jostled one another as they fought for leadership of the pack. Using the glasses for a second, Slocum recognized Clay Barrett as the lead rider. To his surprise, he also recognized a second man, in the middle of the pack. It seemed that this was an important enough mission to require the presence of none other than Abel Bradley himself.

19

Slocum counted six men. Other than Barrett and Bradley, he recognized none of them. Carter raised his rifle, but Slocum knocked it away.

"As long as they don't know we're here, nobody has to get shot," Slocum said.

Carter mumbled angrily, but he left the carbine on the floor of the loft. They watched anxiously as Clay Barrett and another man dismounted. Bradley cupped hands to his mouth and hollered, "Slocum, I know you're in there. Come on out. I give you my word that Carter and the girl won't be harmed. Slocum?"

Barrett entered the house with his gun drawn. The second man, carrying a shotgun, followed him in. Slocum waited patiently. He was certain they would look in the barn, but hoped they wouldn't be too thorough.

Bradley turned in the saddle and looked toward the barn. He nudged his horse alongside one of the other riders. "Check the barn, would you, Pete." Carter inhaled sharply, reaching again for the carbine.

"Wait!" Slocum hissed. "They don't know we're here." He grabbed Randy's arm, and he felt the trembling. Sissy shifted nervously behind him. He turned to look at her. Unlike Randy, she seemed perfectly calm. A carbine balanced across her knees, she seemed to be thinking about something removed in time and space. Her eyes had a vacant look he had seen once before, the preceding night.

Pete kicked his horse toward the barn, dismounting just below them. The two men ducked down and held their breaths. The creak of the barn door seemed impossibly loud. Pete's spurs clinked as he stepped into the barn. They heard him walk into the back, then his boots on the ladder to the loft.

"Pete, you find anything?" Bradley hollered.

Pete jumped back to the floor. "Nope, the stalls are empty," he called. A moment later, he reappeared below the loft door. Slocum watched him mount up while pressing Randy to the floor with one hand.

"I'd expect no better from a coward like Slocum," Bradley said. "He must have left yesterday, straight from the prison."

Barrett stepped back out of the house, his shotgun-toting companion right behind him. Slocum let his breath out in a slow whistle. Both men remounted, and Slocum waited expectantly.

The big deputy wheeled his horse in a circle, reaching behind him for something in his saddlebags.

"What the hell's he doing," Carter whispered.

"I don't know," Slocum answered.

Randy stood up and sprinted toward the loft ladder. Slocum turned to grab him, but missed. He couldn't call out without alerting Bradley and the others. He watched Randy scamper down the ladder, then turned back to the house. Barrett urged his horse forward with his knees. A thin curl of black smoke twined around his shoulders as the horse climbed onto the porch.

Barrett's hands were obscured by his body, but Slocum

heard breaking glass, and he knew what was happening. The horse whinnied and backed off the porch. Barrett disappeared around the corner of the house as Sissy dropped down beside Slocum.

"My God," she said, as the kitchen curtains burst into flame, "the bastard's torching the house."

She got to her feet, but Slocum grabbed her by the back of her belt and hauled her down. "Stay here, and keep down," he said, scrambling toward the ladder.

Randy was already headed for the door as Slocum began his descent. When he hit the floor, Randy was charging into the open. Beyond the young farmer, Slocum saw thick columns of smoke swirling skyward.

"You bastards," Carter hollered, raising his carbine. He fired once, then again. Slocum heard the frightened horses, then another shot.

Carter fell as Slocum burst through the open door, the Colt Navy in his hand. Barrett, the blazing torch still clutched in one hand, charged toward the fallen farmer, his revolver still smoking. His horse skidded to a halt a few feet from Carter and Barrett drew a bead on Randy's broad back.

"Barrett!" Slocum barked. "Don't . . ."

Barrett spun around in the saddle. He looked surprised as he realized who had called to him. He raised his revolver but Slocum fired first. The bullet slammed into Barrett's forehead, knocking him from the saddle. Slocum turned and fired again, this time wounding the shotgunner. The big Remington clattered to the hard ground, and the man slumped in his saddle, clutching his shoulder.

"Nobody move a muscle," Slocum shouted. "Not one!" A skinny, birdlike man with a drooping mustache twitched nervously, and Slocum brought the Colt around. "Hoist 'em, all of you."

Bradley's horse skittered to the side, and he brought his hands down to grab the reins before raising them high over his head. "You won't get away with this, Slocum. You'll hang."

"The hell he will."

Bradley seemed puzzled, and turned to see who had spoken. Slocum, too, was baffled. He heard the sound of a shell being levered into a carbine's chamber.

Two horsemen appeared around the corner of the house. The first rider, a tall man in clothes that showed the trail dust of some hard riding, trained a carbine on Bradley and his men. Slocum noticed the all-too-familiar star of a federal marshal pinned to the man's pocket.

"Who the hell are you?" Bradley demanded. "And what right do you have to interfere here?"

"The name's Clayton, Tom Clayton. *Marshal* Tom Clayton. You fellers, grab some buckets and put that fire out. Now!"

He waited while the men dismounted and ran to the barn. They reappeared a moment later with a half-dozen pails and formed a bucket brigade. They started scooping water from the nearest irrigation ditch. When they settled into a rhythm, Clayton turned back to the judge.

With a sardonic grin, he said, "And I got a little piece of paper here that'll tell you all you need to know about my rights. And yours, for that matter." He stared at Bradley a long moment, then nudged his horse forward again, stopping just to Bradley's left. He stuffed the paper in Bradley's outstretched hand.

"That there's a court order, Judge. Signed by Judge Peterson, up in Prescott. Until further notice, you are ordered to step down from the bench. I'll be in charge here, pending an investigation."

"For what?" Bradley spluttered. "Investigation of what?"

Clayton nodded toward the judge's outstretched hand. "It's all there, in the papers."

"You have no right," Bradley repeated.

"I got all the right I need. It's all legal. Something you

can appreciate, seein' how you're a judge and all. I got another one, too. For Clay Barrett. I don't suppose he's here, is he?"

"Not anymore," Slocum said.

Clayton turned back to him.

Slocum indicated the dead deputy on the ground. "That's Barrett." He walked to Randy Carter and dropped to one knee. Tearing a sleeve from Carter's shirt, he knotted it around the farmer's thigh. He stuck the barrel of Carter's revolver through the loose loop and twisted it, making a crude tourniquet.

Clayton studied him for a long time before speaking. "And who might you be?"

"That there's Slocum, Marshal." The speaker was the second rider. Owen Reilly dismounted and walked to Randy Carter, still writhing on the ground. "He's the one I told you about. The one Barrett framed."

"You live around here, Slocum?" Clayton asked.

"He's a stranger, Marshal," Reilly said. "I already told you that."

"I was talkin' to Slocum, Mr. Reilly. Let him talk for himself."

"Sorry, Marshal."

The fire was out now, and the men returned to their horses. The air was full of the acrid stench of charred wood and burnt cloth.

Clayton waited patiently, letting his eyes flick in Sissy's direction for an instant as she rushed out of the barn to kneel by her brother. "Well?"

"No, sir, I don't live around here, Mr. Clayton. I'm from Georgia, originally. Anyplace I can get work, lately."

"I know what you mean. Tennessee, myself. Until the war. I was at Stone Mountain. That's about all I know about Georgia."

"If you were there, I don't suppose you care to go back."

Clayton grunted. "Not in this life."

Turning back to Bradley, Clayton waved a hand. "Gents," he said, "I suggest you all go back home. Judge, I'll want to see you tomorrow morning. Sheriff Millburn's office. Nine o'clock."

"Sheriff Millburn is dead," Bradley said.

"I know that," Clayton snapped. "Ray was a friend of mine. You might say that's why I got a particular interest in what's going on, at least according to Mr. Reilly, here, and the petition he brought up to Prescott."

Bradley whirled and rode off, the other men following him without a backward glance. Clayton stared after the judge for a few seconds, looked at Barrett's corpse, then at Slocum. "Fellow don't care much for you, you can't do nothing for him no more."

Slocum nodded. "I'll bury him."

"I'd be obliged. I'll want to be talking to you, too. And Mr. Carter. Sheriff's office tomorrow. Ten o'clock." He tilted his head to one side, as if he were studying Slocum's face.

"We'll be there, Marshal."

"I expect you better be. I want to get to the bottom of this mess as soon as I can. Prescott ain't heaven, but it sure as hell has this place beat. I'd like to get back."

Slocum watched the marshal ride off. Owen Reilly grinned at him. "Guess I got here just in time, Mr. Slocum."

"You can say that again, Mr. Reilly."

"Never realized what you was gettin' for your buck, did you." He laughed.

"I guess you could say it was a bargain," Slocum said. He grinned at the old man.

"I'll give you a hand with Randy there. He's gonna need some rest."

Together, they carried Randy into the farmhouse. Sissy hovered behind them like a frightened bird, while Slocum loosened the tourniquet and ripped the pantleg away. He was relieved to see that the wound was relatively minor. It was a long crease in the fleshy part of the thigh, painful but not life-threatening.

Sissy kept wringing her hands, and moaning to herself. Slocum dressed the wound, smearing it with an herbal paste and wrapping a compression bandage in place. Reilly, satisfied that he was no longer needed, took his leave.

With Randy safely attended to, Slocum put Sissy to bed. She had been through a grueling few days and was clearly exhausted. He set up a cot for her alongside Randy's bed. She drifted off almost as soon as she lay down.

Slocum ripped the charred tatters of the curtains and shuffled some furniture to block the broken windows. Satisfied that he had done enough for one day, he spread a heavy blanket on Sissy's bed. Unbuckling his gunbelt, he curled the belt around the holster and set it on the small oak dressing table alongside the bed.

He extinguished the lamp and lay down. His clothes were stiff, and he couldn't get comfortable. Sitting up, Slocum stared out of the window for a while, watching the advancing bleach of the sunlight. The landscape turned the dull sheen of dying leaves. Even the plants lost their green.

Slocum turned away from the window and stripped off his clothes. He caught a glimpse of himself in the aging mirror of Sissy's wardrobe. In the harsh light, he didn't recognize his own body. He wondered if he had changed that much, or if the light and mirror combined to play tricks on him. His own flesh, more ghostly than substantial, seemed to shimmer, as if it were melting from his bones.

Slocum suppressed a shudder and dropped back to the bed. Cupping his hands behind his head, he watched the blocks of sunlight march across the floor. He was tired, but he wouldn't let himself sleep.

It wasn't Bradley that kept him awake, it was the way

Clayton had looked at him. The marshal's eyes had bored right into him, as if they were drilling test holes, looking for something his lawman's instinct told him was hidden there. Slocum had seen that look before, and had met more than one lawman who had the uncanny ability.

Part of him wanted to run, and part of him wouldn't permit it. Barrett was dead, but that was only half the battle. The larger part of the cancer still remained. Bradley had to be cut out of Flat Creek or the town would never survive.

As the sun began to set, he could no longer keep his eyes open. He tugged a blanket up over his shoulders and curled into a restless sleep. He tossed and turned, waking often, seeing things move in the shadows, hearing noises in the dark. He wanted to get up, but his body was nearly drained. He let himself drift off again and again, like a man with a deadly fever, afraid that each sleep will be his last, too weak to do anything but let it happen.

Once, he saw the moon, closer to full now, through the unbroken window, but failed to recognize it. Looking at it upside down, he tried to understand what it was. When the puzzle proved too much for him, he closed his eyes rather than continue to struggle.

A sound in the kitchen awakened him. He listened for a minute, slipping the Colt from his holster. A dull orange glow approached the doorway, slowly brightening the walls of the narrow hallway. He brought the Colt up, aiming waist high through the center of the doorway.

Slocum saw the lamp before he saw anything else. What he saw next was anything but what he had been prepared for. Holding the lamp as if it were a priest's censer, letting it swing gently back and forth with each step, Sissy Carter walked through the doorway.

Her long black hair glittered, held in place by a single silver comb over one ear. It was the only thing she wore. She paused, as if waiting for him to catch his breath. She looked that good, and every movement of her body told him that she knew it. The full breasts, their nipples already erect at the hearts of shadowy areolae, swayed gently as she walked.

Her long legs were wrapped in flames where the orange glow of the lantern was reflected by her oiled skin. Tiny droplets of water clung to the coal-black triangle nestled between her thighs, sparkling like a night full of orange stars. She moved easily, with an unsuspected grace. Slocum caught himself staring at the floor, as if to be certain her feet actually touched the rough wood beneath them.

He let the gun fall to the floor. He felt himself stirring, his cock wriggling against his leg like a live thing before standing up on its own. Sissy hung the lantern from an overhead hook. The line from her breast to her extended hand seemed to stretch out to infinity. Her movements were exaggeratedly slow, each ripple of muscle accenting the contours of her perfectly sculpted flesh.

One hand went between her legs as she let go of the lantern, and with the other she placed a finger to her lips. Sissy moved onto the bed, still having said nothing. She stood over him, straddling his legs with her own. Sinking forward onto her knees, she reached down to hold him upright as she impaled herself.

Already slippery, she let her weight do the work, lowering herself onto him with practiced ease. He reached up and took her breasts in his hands as she leaned slightly forward. He raised his head, still half asleep. Her oiled body caught fire from the lantern dangling overhead. Each twist and turn as she swiveled her hips and threw her head back painted her with light and rainbows.

Sissy moaned, an animal sound that started deep in her throat and clawed its way out. Slocum held her hips, his hands slipping on the smooth, slick satin of her skin. She bent forward, teasing him with her breasts, dangling just out of reach of his lips. He heard a voice, and it took him a moment to realize it wasn't Sissy's.

He looked past Sissy toward the door. There, framed between a ripe breast and a shiny hip, gun in hand, stood Karen Alston.

"And I thought you were a one-woman kinda guy," she grinned. "For shame, Slocum, for shame."

20

Karen closed the door. She looked at Sissy with a lopsided smile. "Don't stop on my account, honey," she said. "A girl finds a good horse, she ought to ride him as often as she can."

Sissy cursed, but made no move to get up. Slocum was beyond embarrassment. He kept his eyes on the gun. He felt Sissy working him, and shifted his weight, trying to slide out from under her.

Karen reached for the buttons on her shirt, still keeping the gun trained on Slocum. With one hand, she tugged the shirt out of her belt, then slipped it off one arm. Shifting the gun, she tugged the other sleeve free and let the shirt fall to the floor. Unbuckling her riding skirt, she let it fall around her ankles. Gracefully, she stepped free, now wearing only her boots.

"What do you think, Slocum?" she asked. She twirled around like a flamenco dancer, then walked toward the bed. The boot heels rapping on the floor were the only sound in the small room.

"What do you want?" Slocum asked.

"I don't know. Maybe the same thing your girlfriend there wants. Maybe something else altogether. Maybe even both."

Sissy pulled away. The sticky juices binding her to Slocum gurgled as their bodies separated. Karen laughed.

"You're disgusting," Sissy whispered.

"Just honest, honey. Take my word for it, it's better that way."

Sissy moved toward the door, cradling her breasts in crossed arms in an effort to cover them. Karen eyed her appraisingly. "Not bad," she said. Then, to Slocum, "You have good taste."

Sissy yanked the door open, the last shreds of her dignity blowing away in the breeze. She slammed the door closed.

"Stay right there, cowboy," Karen said. She glided toward the bed. Raising one leg, she climbed on, straddling Slocum. His erection had returned, and Karen gripped the slippery shaft in one hand, stroking it slowly, almost meditatively. Satisfied that it was hard enough to suit her, she let her fingers linger a moment on its head. She arched her hips and bent his cock forward. With a sudden snap of her hips, she took him all the way in.

"Wetter *is* better," she grinned. Still holding the gun, she stroked Slocum's chest with one long nail. The tip of her tongue darted to one corner of her mouth, and she started to rock. "You wanted to know the whole story," she panted. "I'll tell you in a little while."

Slocum grabbed the wrist of her gun hand, twisting it until the revolver fell onto the bedclothes. He grabbed the pistol and slid out from under her. The move had caught her by surprise.

"Hey, why'd you do that?" Despite the fullness of her figure, she looked like nothing so much as a spoiled little girl. "I thought you liked me."

"I don't know what to think about you, Karen. I can't

believe anything you say. If you told me the sky was blue, I'd have to go outside and check."

Slocum got off the bed and bent to retrieve her clothes. He tossed them to her without looking at her. "Get dressed," he snapped. "Then, if you still want to tell me anything, maybe I'll listen."

Slocum slipped his pants on, then buckled his gunbelt around his waist. He sat down on a chair to put on his socks, then yanked his boots on and stood up to stamp them tight.

Karen sat on the bed, her legs folded beneath her. She held the clothes in a loose ball in her lap. "I guess I lose this round, Slocum," she said. She stared at her clothes, the fingers of one hand fussing aimlessly with the wrinkled shirt.

"Is that what this is to you, a game?" He shook his head, half disgusted and half amazed. "You know Clay Barrett is dead, don't you?"

"Yes."

"Then do you mind telling me what the hell is going on?"

"Yes, I mind. Hell yes, I do."

"Then get out of here, and don't come back."

"I didn't say I wouldn't tell you. All I said was I minded."

Slocum stepped toward her, torn between her helplessness and anger at the way she had used him. She looked up at him, and there were tears in her eyes. She patted the mattress with one hand. "Sit down, please, sit down."

Slocum did as she asked. She let her head rest on his shoulder, and he put his arm around her in their first chaste embrace.

"Promised Land Ranch, that's the judge's ranch, wasn't always his, isn't now, not really. It belonged to my father, too, the judge's brother."

"You mean Bradley is your uncle?" Slocum was incredulous.

"Yes. When Daddy died, he left his share to me. I already told you that the judge was trustee. He wanted to build it up. At first he just bought people out. But he got greedy. When people wouldn't sell, he started to pressure them. The bigger the ranch got, the easier it was. But he knew there was no future in owning half the desert. He needed something to make it livable, to connect it with the rest of the world."

"That's where the prison came in."

"Not at first. That was Barrett's idea."

"But the judge went along with it."

"Yes. Barrett convinced him that cheap labor was the only solution. The railroads weren't interested in expanding into the high desert. They didn't believe it would pay."

"So the judge decided to do it himself. What about your name, where does the Alston come from?"

"My husband."

"You're married?"

"No, not anymore. Will died back east. I had been at school. I got married without permission, but there was nothing anyone could do about it. I didn't care. I hated it here anyway, especially after Daddy died. But, when Will died . . . I . . . ." She choked off a sob.

Slocum patted her shoulder, then began to massage the back of her neck. He reached into her lap and tugged the shirt free and draped it around her shoulders.

"I'm all right," she said. "Anyway, I had no place to turn, no family, except the judge. Mama died when I was eight. The judge told me I would have to earn my share of the ranch. I didn't have any choice, really."

"So you sold yourself to cowboys on the move. You set them up for a few weeks on the work gang."

Karen swallowed hard. It was difficult for her to continue, but she was determined to tell it all. "It wasn't easy, but I got used to it. I mean, I didn't know those men. They meant nothing to me. As far as I knew, they meant nothing to anyone. But then Clay Barrett wasn't satisfied. He started to act like he owned me. He started to visit me nights when I wasn't working. Pretty soon, it was almost every night. It was too late for me to get out."

"You could have run away."

"How? Where would I go?"

"You could have told the sheriff what was going on."

"I did. At first, I was scared. The judge told me I was an accomplice, that if I turned him in, I would go to jail myself. I couldn't stand that. But I couldn't continue, so I told Sheriff Millburn. I told him everything. He didn't want to believe me, not at first, but I made him see what was going on. That's when he went to Prescott. He was going to get the marshal down here . . . only he never made it."

"Barrett?"

She nodded. "You've got to help me, Slocum. I know I have no right to ask you, but I don't know where else to turn."

"How can I help? The marshal is here, the territorial authorities know what's going on. It's all over, Karen. You're free."

She shook her head. "No . . . the judge, he won't let anything stop him. He's got friends in Prescott, he's got the money to buy whoever doesn't owe him a favor. He's, I mean . . ."

"Look, Karen, if the marshal can't stop him, what can I do?"

"There's only one way to stop him." Karen tilted her head back, and Slocum found himself staring into eyes so deep he thought he might drown in them if he looked too long. "Will you help me, Slocum, please?"

"No. I'm not a hired gun. I don't kill people I don't even know, and for no reason. I had enough of that in the war."

"I can make it worth your while. If the judge dies, I'll be a very wealthy woman, one of the wealthiest in the territory. And you already know what else I can do for you.

Remember?" She tossed the shirt off her shoulders, but Slocum stood up as she reached for him.

"Forget it," Slocum snapped. "I don't kill people for money. And I sure as hell won't kill someone for a free fuck, no matter how good it is."

"It was good, wasn't it?" She licked her lips, but Slocum turned away.

"Get out of here before I shoot *you*," he whispered.

She stood up and threw her clothes on. "You'll regret this, Slocum. I swear to God, you'll regret it."

"It won't be the first thing I regret. And probably not the last, either." Slocum opened the door and stepped into the small hallway. Sissy, dressed in jeans and a shirt, was leaning against the wall.

He ignored her and walked on out into the early morning. The moon was almost down, sitting on the edge of the distant mountains like a silver comma. He walked to the barn, then remembered that the horses were still hobbled downstream. He walked back to the house just as Karen, her shirt on but still open, brushed past Sissy and walked out onto the porch.

She stormed past him without a word, and he stepped inside. He got his shirt and hat, then went for the horses. When he returned, riding the big roan and trailing the other two, Sissy was sitting on the porch. He rode to the barn, and she followed him in. He dismounted and began to remove the reins and saddles of the Carter horses.

He draped the saddles and blankets over a stall railing, and urged the horses into their stalls. Grabbing a pitchfork, he tossed some hay into each stall. As he worked, he was conscious of Sissy's eyes on his back, following his every move. He felt his shoulders tense for the question he knew was coming.

When he finished with their horses, he tossed a little hay in front of the big roan, but left the saddle and reins in place.

"You're leaving, aren't you?" Sissy asked. Her voice

was so soft, he wasn't sure he heard the question.

Without looking at her, he nodded. "Yes, I am."

"Why?"

"It's time, that's all."

"Don't you want to see this through to the end?"

"There's nothing more I can do. What difference does it make?"

"You already know the answer to that."

"No, I don't."

"You're a coward, Slocum, plain and simple. What are you running away from."

Before answering, he thought about the look in Tom Clayton's eyes. "Maybe myself," he whispered. "Maybe nothing at all."

"Bullshit!"

"All the same . . . I'm goin'."

He whirled on her. "Look, Sissy, you don't know me. You don't know anything about me."

"I know more than you think. I know you have something to hide. I can see it in your face. For Christ's sake, I could feel it in bed with you. The way you held back, trying to keep part of you hidden even then, even inside me, you were running away."

Slocum shrugged. "You know what you know, you feel what you feel. That's fine. Why don't you allow me to do the same, all right? End of discussion." He stepped past her, shaking off the hand she laid on his arm. "No, Sissy, just no."

"Are you at least going to tell Randy? The least you can do is wait until he wakes up."

"I'll wait a little while," he said. "But at sunup, I'm moving on." He walked to the house and gathered the rest of his gear. Sissy watched him silently. When he was finished, Randy Carter stood in the doorway of his bedroom. He looked pale, and the bloody bandage on his leg accented the sickly pallor.

"You're leaving, I guess."

"Yup."

"You sure about it?"

"Unh-huh."

"I guess there's nothing I can say, is there?"

"Nope."

"Is there anything I can help you with? Some problem, maybe."

Slocum shook his head. "Look, Randy, you helped me once, and got your ass in a sling. I appreciate it, but I'm not about to ask you for help that wouldn't do any good. There's nothing you can do for me that I can't do for myself."

"Fair enough." He hobbled across the room and took Slocum's hand firmly in his own. "Good luck. But if you change your mind, the offer's open. Anytime."

"I appreciate that." Slocum stepped out onto the porch as the sun was coming up.

Sissy was waiting for him in the barn. "I know why you're leaving," she said. "I finally figured it out."

"Oh really?" Slocum was surprised. "Why's that?"

"It's Karen. You like her better than you like me. Am I right?"

"No, you're not right. That's ridiculous."

"Yes, yes it is right. I don't see why that slut is more important to you than I am. I mean, after all, she's . . . well, you know. What she is, I mean."

"Oh, and what exactly is she?"

"She's a whore, for Christ's sake. She fucked you for money. And you don't even see the difference."

"Frankly, I don't. You're right about that," Slocum snapped. "As I remember it, you asked me to kill Clay Barrett after our little roll in the hay. What's the difference —money, favors? Sex in exchange for either. It's commerce, Sissy. That's what it is. And that's why there's no difference between you and Karen."

"You fucking bastard!" Sissy slapped him as hard as she

could. He let her land the first blow, then grabbed her wrist.

"Don't blame me for telling you the truth, Sissy. I'm right, and you know it. That's why you're angry. You don't want to face the truth. But it's there, all the same." He swung into the saddle. "In fact," he said, jerking the reins, "you're even better at it than Karen. After all, Clay Barrett's dead, just like you wanted. I never gave Karen a cent."

If she said anything, the roan's hooves drowned it out.

21

Slocum stared at the rising sun, trying to decide which way to go. All roads led to Flat Creek. So all roads led away. Any one would be fine with him. He kicked the roan into a trot, heading down along the creek. Prescott no longer seemed a good place to go, with Clayton at least uneasy, if not outright suspicious.

"Maybe Tucson," Slocum whispered half aloud.

He knew he could follow Flat Creek for a while, until it intersected with the Salt River. From there, he would have to cross the Superstition Range, but then he could skirt the San Pedro River almost all the way. Water wouldn't be a problem. Once there, he could decide what to do with the rest of his life. He smiled at the thought, realizing he drew that conclusion once or twice a month, and once or twice a month he chewed himself out for making lousy decisions.

He looked back over his shoulder, and Sissy was still watching him, hands on hips, those long, long legs slightly spread and planted firmly in the yard.

Beyond the house, something seemed to be stirring up

the dust. A cloud, picking up a fiery red tint from the sun, boiled above the thin stand of trees lining Flat Creek. From the size of it, two or three horses were approaching, and their riders were in a hurry.

His first thought was that Clayton had seen a poster, or otherwise been alerted that Slocum was not exactly a choirboy. But when he considered the possibility, it didn't seem too likely that Clayton would bother to come all the way out there. He was, after all, expecting to see Slocum that morning, at ten o'clock.

Slocum urged the roan into a full gallop, anxious to put a little distance between himself and the Carter farm. Clayton had his hands full with a lot more important matters than checking out a chance encounter with a man who might be on a wanted poster. If he was looking for Slocum, and found him gone, there was no way Clayton would bother coming after him.

Glancing back at the roiling cloud, like bloody smoke just above the horizon, something told Slocum to go back. There was unfinished business here, he knew it, and he hadn't wanted to face up to the fact. But there comes a time when a man has to see something through, no matter how painful it might be for him.

He had started something in Flat Creek, stirred up a hornet's nest, without even realizing it. But the worst thing about hornets is that they don't give a damn about your motive. You stir them up, and somebody has to pay the consequences. If they can't get you, they'll take the next best thing. It was true that he could ride away. But it was also true that he'd be looking over his shoulder the rest of his life, because a man like Abel Bradley, the Bible-thumping hypocrite, doesn't lose easily. As long as he had a dollar in his pocket and a breath in his lungs, he'd be thinking about Slocum, wondering where he was, and how he could get to him. That was something Slocum didn't need. It was better to finish it, here and now.

In a way, Sissy had been right: he *did* owe Randy something. He had been the one to kick the hornets' nest. He couldn't leave Carter and Reilly and the rest of the people, no matter how scared they might be, and how contemptuous of that fear he might be, to the vengeance of Abel Bradley.

Slocum pulled up and stood in the stirrups. Over the relatively flat terrain, he could still make out the roof of Carter's barn. The cloud had begun to dissipate. The riders must have stopped at the Carter farm. Wheeling the roan in a tight circle, he dug his spurs into its flanks. The big stallion leaped forward. He could feel the power of its huge body as the horse hit a full gallop.

As he approached, Slocum could hear angry voices. He broke into the open just as Abel Bradley swung an open palm at Sissy. She tried to duck away, but Bradley caught her by the hair and threw her to the ground. Two more men, still on horseback, sat by, grinning broadly. He had been wrong about its being Marshal Clayton, and he had been wrong about the number of horses, too. A fourth rider sat behind the two cowboys, hands tied to the saddle horn.

Karen Alston looked as if she had already received a dose of the same justice Bradley was preparing to administer to Sissy Carter.

The judge heard the hoofbeats and turned. Tossing his long coattail behind him, he reached for his revolver. Slocum drew the Colt Navy but held his fire. Bradley wrestled Sissy to her feet and used her body as a shield. He backed toward his horse, one arm squeezing Sissy's throat.

One of the mounted cowboys, the same birdlike man Slocum had wounded in their last confrontation, drew his pistol, a Colt Peacemaker, and aimed it at Karen.

"You was running, wasn't you, Slocum? I knew I was right about you. You're gutless. But I had a trump card, didn't I?"

"What might that be, Judge," Slocum drawled.

"Like most sinners, most particularly fornicators, you are a victim of woman's flesh. It's like a disease with you.

Karen was right." The judge glanced over his shoulder at Karen Alston. It looked like he was grinning.

"Judge, I think you better let the women go. You don't want to give Marshal Clayton anything else to think about, do you?"

Bradley laughed. "Clayton isn't thinking about anything. Not anymore."

Slocum nodded. "You backshoot him, too, like you did the sheriff?"

"That was Barrett done that. He shot Millburn, not me."

"Maybe so, but it was your idea. What about this time? You have the guts to pull the trigger yourself, or did you get somebody else to do your dirty work?"

Bradley snarled. "You talk big, Slocum, but you're nothing. You're nobody. Do you have any idea what you're dealing with here? Do you know how powerful I am?"

"I don't give a shit about you *or* your so-called power. Bradley, you're about as frightening as a dead snake, which is what you're gonna be in one minute, unless you let those women go."

"You don't get it, do you, Slocum? You just don't get it. 'Vengeance is mine, saith the Lord.' And I aim to do the Lord's work, Slocum. Right now, here, this morning."

From the corner of his eye, Slocum saw Randy Carter, using a carbine as a crutch, hobbling past the corner of the farmhouse. So far, Bradley and his henchmen hadn't noticed him, but he had to cover another fifteen yards before he'd be in position to get the drop on the judge. Somehow, Slocum had to keep Bradley talking.

"Judge, I'll make you a deal."

"What kind of deal?"

"How about you and me ride up to Prescott together. We'll tell our stories to the territorial governor and see who's right. See, Judge, your problem is—"

Bradley cut him off. "I don't have a problem, Slocum, you do."

Slocum ignored the interruption. "Your problem is that

you've been having your own way so long, you don't even know what's right and wrong anymore. The way you see it, if it's good for you, it must be right. If it's bad for you, it must be wrong. Now that isn't how a judge is supposed to see things, is it?"

"What do you know about a judge's work? What do you know about the awful burdens, and the awful power necessary to bear those burdens?"

"You know what Luke says: 'Out of thine own mouth will I judge thee.'"

"Don't you dare quote Scriptures at me, you heathen." Bradley was getting irritated. He seemed to be on the verge of exploding. Slocum bit his lower lip, watching Randy Carter's painful progress. Another ten feet ought to do it.

Slocum sighed. "All right, Judge, suppose you tell me what you want."

"What I want, what I want. Why, Slocum, I'm surprised. I thought you knew. I want justice, simple justice."

"Justice for who?"

"For Flat Creek and its citizens, whom else."

"What's that got to do with us?"

"That's for me to decide."

Carter was in position, but he couldn't hold the gun steady. Slocum wriggled his fingers, and Carter nodded. He knelt down, trained the carbine on Bradley, and levered a round into the chamber. Bradley heard the click and turned.

"Let her go, Judge," Slocum said. Bradley seemed confused. He swiveled his head back and forth between Carter and Slocum. "Let her go now."

"You fellows," Carter shouted. "Throw your guns down."

The two cowboys looked at Bradley. "Don't do it. He won't shoot."

Sissy brought her boot heel down sharply on Bradley's instep. He howled, and Sissy broke free. "All right, Judge, it's over. Throw down your gun and tell your men to do the same." Slocum stepped toward him, the Colt steady in his hand. "Do it!"

The two gunmen, staring down the muzzle of Carter's Winchester, tossed their guns on the ground.

Bradley turned, his lips twisted. A thin sheet of spittle, almost like foam, arced through the air as he turned back to Slocum. "Never! You can't, you won't..." The words were almost a howl. He swung his revolver and Slocum fired. The heavy Colt slug slammed into Bradley's shoulder and he reeled backwards. He stepped on one of the discarded pistols and his feet went out from under him.

As he fell, the judge brought his own gun up and Slocum fired again. This time, the shot struck Bradley under the chin, breaking his jaw and burying itself in his cheek. He continued to snarl, spitting bloody froth. "I am the law here. I am the law here. You can't do this. I am the law here."

Again he raised the pistol, his eyes bulging in fury. He fired wildly, the gun bucking in his fist. He fired twice more, the second shot whining just past Slocum's ear.

Slocum aimed and fired. The shot slammed into Bradley's contorting body with a heavy thud. The judge arced like a trout trying to shake a hook, supported by head and heels only. He groaned and collapsed in a heap. Then he lay still.

Slocum turned to the two gunmen. "It's over, gents. You'd best move on. You see anybody who doesn't believe it's over, you make sure they understand just how over it is. Now git."

Slocum walked to the horse and reached up to untie Karen's hands. "You all right?" he asked.

She nodded.

He walked back to his own horse and swung into the saddle. Without a word, he sawed on the reins and swung the big roan around, toward Tucson.

He heard Sissy calling after him, but he ignored her, trying hard not to hear what she was saying. The hoofbeats behind him were another matter. He slowed the roan to a walk and waited. Karen Alston pulled up alongside him.

"Where are you going?" It was half demand and half question. "It's over. You said so yourself. Why are you leaving?"

"Without looking at her, he said, "You know the answer to that as well as I do."

"But I thought that we—"

"Karen, you got what you wanted. The judge is dead. Promised Land is yours."

"But I want you, Slocum. We can work the ranch together. We can build it up even more. We can finish the railroad. It'll be a gold mine, Slocum. Don't you understand?"

Slocum spurred the big roan. Without turning, he tossed over his shoulder, "You sound just like the judge."

"Slocum, you bastard."

He didn't answer.

JAKE LOGAN